RIDERSHIP

B.RANDOM

WORDWORM PRESS

A CPI catalogue record for this book is available from the British Library.

ISBN: 9781999724658
Published by Wordworm Press
First edition

To

Charlie

MRAX

Hy!,

BOOK 3

Brandon

For my Rovers.

Read the Series:

BEFORE...

Mrax is a distant planet saved from its destructive orbit by the heroic efforts of the Mraxi together with the half-Mraxi boy they recruited. Ky, brought up human, thrust unprepared into their ambitious scheme, has to learn to master alien skills to succeed.

Mraxi are a race that age slowly. Their human appearance differs only from ours by a thin black stripe that extends down one side of their neck and down their body. Mraxi shrink and fade in stages over centuries to withered, frail creatures which ultimately reduce to the size of a pea, when they emit green light. Their mental abilities grow and broaden with no impairment from age.

With the sudden change in orbit, Mrax's pristine environment is in chaos. Cities and safety are gone. Earthquakes, freak weather and hungry, lethal creatures   abound...

1

⁝Run⁝

Ky twitched, anxious eyes scanning for movement between the crowding alien trees. Only his mrug drifted lazy circles above, a manta-ray silhouette in the sky, watching him.

'We really need to go.' He urged, not daring to make a sound. It was great they could always talk mind to mind. He felt less alone.

Fay, his best friend, tossed another pebble into the stream. Her pale mrug crept from the water on its crawlers, the two fat tentacles on its back waving. Its huge scarlet eyes watched him too, flicking up to its scarred cousin in the sky as it climbed slowly to her ankle, wrapping its wings around tight.

Fay didn't budge.

'Relax will you?' Her voice rang in his head.

Gritting his teeth, he glanced at her, ready to snap back.

Suddenly he couldn't breathe. Her narrow face was in shadow. Screaming memories came flooding back.2

Chilled, he peered up. A flock of bright flyers flashed, shrieking in the glooming trees.

'The sun's going down. One more stone, then we need to get back.' Straining for every sound, Ky wagged a hopeful pebble from the

bank.

'It's lovely here. So good to get away from the clinic…' She sighed, accepting his gift.

It was, but not now.

A loud chirruping started up nearby. Ky tapped the record setting on his phone.

'You know we have to go.' Ky fidgeted, sucking his lip.

'Being out after dark's one of the few things I miss about Earth.' She flung her stone into the river.

Suddenly all flyersong stopped. Ky's mouth dried up. He flicked the phone off.

The plop rang loud in the silence.

Fay jerked upright. She scrambled to her feet, whipping her head around.

'Get up!' Staring into the trees, she flapped a hand.

He was already up, heart thumping. How he hated being right.

On the balls of his feet, Ky peered into the shadow-filled trees, chewing his cheek.

3

He called his mrug back from feeding. As usual, it ignored him.

Jamming his phone deeper into the shallow Mraxi pocket, he bounced.

A tall tree shivered, shaking off a drift of fiery leaves.

They both jumped at a crack like a gunshot.

'There.' Fay pointed. A thick branch swung down. Something big moved behind it.

'Run!' Ky took off, plunging breathless into the undergrowth.

'Don't ping!' Fay screamed in his head.

Feet flying, he felt the phone slip from his pocket, daren't stop.

Fay leapt beside him up the slope, hair bows bobbing targets in the sudden twilight.

Twigs and leaves slapped his face. Roots snagged his feet.

'Why can't I ping somewhere else right now?' He sent, even if it did give you creepy

chills.

All he could hear was the monster's smashing, crashing progress as it drew closer.

He burst into a glade, unanswered.

Spotting a hollow log, he dived in, sure he could feel its hot breath on the back of his neck.

'Fay? I lost you.' Gasping, he thumped his chest.

Scrambling along on his knees, catching biting bugs in his long hair, he heard it stop.

Not daring to breathe, he froze in the dim tube. His mrug would never find him now.

A crispy rustle started up inside the log. He curled his fists, fighting the urge to scratch.

Heart thumping, he waited, suddenly aware of something slithering against his leg. Every hair stood up on his skin.

Outside, a twig snapped. It was still there.

'Fay?' Any other time he'd be gone.

He felt a small, seeking nose against his leg. Jumping, twisting away in the small space, his feet ground loud on the wood. This wasn't Earth. Here, everything could kill you.

Something scuttled across his face. Before he could stop it, he sneezed.

Panting, he faced the end of the tunnel, muscles locked tight.

The light was blocked by a huge, orange eye. A rank, rumbling roar blasted in, shaking the air.

Ky clapped his hands over his ears, trying not to inhale.

The end of the rotting tunnel exploded. Long claws flashed in the gloom.

Suddenly Ky found himself upside down, flopping helpless over and over in a storm of dirt and crawlers.

The rolling stopped. His hoarse panting filled the air. He scraped a thousand bugs off his skin, spat them out, rubbing his head.

The log began sliding, grinding along the

ground. Fay must have gone. He began to wind up his power, ready to ping.

Shuffling around, dizzy, Ky crawled away from the claws and the dustbin stench snorting in.

Sucking his dry tongue, he watched the clearing slide by. Razor-edged grasses rasped on the bark.

Stark against the peach sky, he saw two flyers swooping into the tops of trees. Tops?

Too late, Ky realised what that meant. Ready to ping, he hesitated, Fay's warning still ringing in his ears.

The log tipped over the cliff.

'Aaah!' Ky slid out into space, running on air.

Falling in slow motion, he squinted at the flashing scales. In a cloud of beast breath, he flailed. Giant claws whipped out to grab him. The monster yowled, missed.

'Dad!'

There was no response. No time.

All he knew was air pushing at the skin

7

B. Random

on his face, long hair streaming up, wind flapping his clothes as tree tops rushed past in a blur...

2

¡Snap¡

Peeking between the sheltering roots of an ancient mingo tree, Fay watched the scaly back glisten. The spikes on its elbows glinted as it reached out to spin the log. As the temperature dropped, dragon breath spiralled up from its treble nostril slits.

'No!' Curling tight, panting, she covered her eyes. Casting out, she felt the depth of its determination, its hunger. She hadn't dreamed this.

At a tortured scraping sound, she peeked through her fingers. Frowning she leaned out between the roots. A bob, long and scaly, scuttled over her hand.

The tmeg's long tail lashed the fragrant sunherb in front of her as it bent to push. A clatter of disturbed spinners blocked her view as the beast flapped long wings, their wind tugging her hair. All she could see was the ridge of spikes on its back shining, straight and golden.

'No!' She leapt from cover, waving her arms.

It continued pushing the log toward the cliff with determined claws. Golden light danced off its flexing muscles.

'Stop!' She scrabbled for a heavy stick and threw it.

The scaly head whipped round. Fay's throat closed. Sword teeth snapped at her streaking shadow. She dived for cover under a cage of roots.

Snorting, it turned back to its task, shoving the log out into space with a flare of its wings. Their blast whipped her hair, stinging her face with a shower of leaves. Behind it, she caught a glimpse of the end of the log tipping up as it fell away.

Ky's mrug spun anxious circles above, the big eyes set through its flat body gazing down.

A yell rang out.

'Ky!' Feeling his shriek slice through her, Fay clapped her hands to her head, catching her nails in dangling fibres.

The ground trembled beneath her, showering more grit.

Another earthquake? She chewed her lip.

Whipping round, the beast snorted. Rumbling low, the tmeg sniffed her out. It scrabbled at the shredded sunherb in front of her, foul breath filling her screaming mouth.

Trapped, she was powerless to help Ky or

herself. She dare not ping away, not if there was a chance of taking it with her. It felt so human.

Another whoosh of wings whipped a sapling that fell under its giant feet. A storm of leaves spiralled up around it.

Unflinching, it rumbled, louder, reaching down. Oh, for the chill luxury of a ping!

The ground shuddered, sprinkling grit. The tmeg staggered, pushing relentless through the roots.

She cowered away from one probing claw. It snagged a tangle, ripping it out.

'Ew,' Fay covered her head in the resulting deluge.

The flapping brought a knotted branch down across its nose. Heedless, it reached in again.

Frantic heels scrabbled to push her back from the seeking claw. She had nowhere to go.

The beast snarled as the world shook

again.

Roots ripped from the soil, Her mingo tree leaned. She shrieked, brushing another shower of bugs away. A crack shuddered open beneath her like a mouth. She hooked her feet into the roots and clung on, whimpering.

The surprised tmeg flapped up, lifting its feet from the ground.

Through shredded roots, she saw it hover for one breathless moment.

Creaking, the mingo tree began to tip, lifting her into view. Her heart stopped. She tugged out her feet, springing for cover

With a thunderous ripping sound, the ground opened up. The crack zipped away into the forest, trees dancing. Leaves flew as they leaned and fell.

Scratching, Fay peeked out beneath a giant leaf. Dare she ping?

Its swirling shadow filled the leaf-litter sky. The world trembled again. The mingo tree crunched down into the undergrowth.

Before she could move, one giant foot crashed down, crushing more sunherb. Its sweet scent flowered around her.

Hope gone, biting her tongue, she jerked back under cover. The thunder of her blood drowned all other sound.

Leaning down, it snorted her sheltering bushes flat.

'Urgh. Go away you stinker!' Exposed, she bellowed at it, throwing dirt into its eye.

The sound of its clacking teeth would ring through her dreams forever.

3

⫶Crack⫶

It felt like crashing to a wet stone floor. Cold choked Ky's lungs, closing like a clamp on his head.

He felt a rock against his feet, kicked off.

Skin burning, he shot through the surface, gasping for breath. Waves spat, jumped and slapped at his face.

Treading water, blinking, he spotted the shore. The mrug plunged in beside him with a happy splash.

His clogged ears made out a snort. The beast stared down, ropes of drool dripping from long fangs. One eye seemed half closed.

Sunset burnished its scales, the spikes on its long neck, bright against the cliff face. It lifted its wings, trumpeting.

Ky yearned for the prickling, cold fizz of a ping. He didn't dare, after Fay's warning.

Teeth chattering, he started to swim. It was harder than the air swimming Dad had taught him. A cracking sensation shot down the stripe from his neck down the side of his chest.

'Ow.' He stopped, startled, thrashing. A large wave smacked him in the mouth.

The pain eased. The chill bit deeper. He couldn't see through the cloudy, angry water. That deadly shadow was sure to strike from above.

Choking, he churned on, standing as soon as he could. Slogging ashore on jelly legs, Ky looked up again.

The beast was half way down the cliff, using those claws, even the tip of its tail, to hang on, fluttering. Rocks seemed to crumble away from its grip, tumbling into the depths.

Any moment he would hear the sail-snap of those wings. It would stoop like a giant hawk, claws out.

His mrug soared up, circling its snapping head. He called it away, ribs aching.

At least if it was chasing him, Fay would be safe.

The cracking feeling stopped. Shaking himself like a dog, rubbing his chest, he leapt back into the trees.

'Dad!' his mind screamed, feet and heart pounding.

There was still no response.

'You're never there for me are you!? Never!' he screeched into the blurring forest.

He heard the splash as it landed. The sound was muffled by the trees; still too close.

He ran, stumbling over creepers, vines,

rocks. Ferns tangled around his legs. Cobwebs like tight elastic tripped him, bounced him off.

The creaking, smashing sounds behind grew louder. Wind howled in the trees. A gust almost pushed him off his feet.

At a creaking moan, he peeked back. A giant tree tilted and fell in a hail of red leaves. Dusk was settling like a million cobwebs, making it hard to see.

Gasping, he concentrated on placing one flying foot after another. The ground seemed to dance under him.

His foot landed on air.

'Aah!'

This time he plunged into warm water, spitting out the taste of eggs.

Not again!

Shaking, he wiped his eyes, dragged back his hair.

Looking up through a small circle of shivering leaves above, he saw the silver moon, Blim, gleaming behind.

Scanning around him in the dimness, the cave walls glowed pink from a thousand tiny ear-shaped fungus, showing him an oval tunnel leading away. His warm bath took up most of the space.

He popped to his feet as something roared, too close.

Heart thudding, he gazed up.

A flying shadow blocked the view, passed. Blim blinded him again.

He waited, listening to the gurgle and drip around him.

That roar came again, distant.

Sighing, he sank back into the steaming water to float. At least he'd be clean, even if he smelled eggy. He connected with his mrug, floating anxious outside. Through its wondrous eyes, he watched the beast swing away, roaring.

Something touched his leg.

He jumped out, couldn't guess what lived down here.

'Dad!'

11

Still there was no reply.

'Waste of time.' Ky ground his teeth, fighting back a host of tender memories and a sob.

Was he any safer right now in the dark unknown, than up there in the moonlit jungle?

4

┊Gobble┊

'Fay? You okay?'

'Of course. I found a cave,' she snapped, panting as she pushed carefully through the creeper. Fists tight in her pockets, she crept further into the pink glow.

'Me too. I see a tunnel. Maybe they connect. I'm going to take a look.'

Fay scanned for life nearby. Sighing, she found nothing but the usual pink fungus coating the walls, jutting like a thousand tiny ears. She doubted she was in the same caves as Ky.

'Be careful.'

'Ha.'

Grimacing, Fay crept deeper into the tomb-like tunnel. All she could hear was the occasional, echoing drip.

'This is fun. I'm enjoying this. Really,' she hissed, her voice bouncing back like a slither off the walls.

He had no idea how much she hated caves and tunnels. All manner of lethal creatures could pounce on you from the dark. Packs of panther-like slinkers could surround you. Giant webbers could block your exit with beautiful, sticky traps. Pombats made giant hives protected by vicious, leathery guards with hooks on their wings and razor claws. She shuddered, searching the roof for signs.

He didn't know, not yet.

Her foot slid in slime. She tumbled to one knee, knocking her arm on the wall.

'Ow.' A chip broke off, complete with fungus, leaving a stripe of pink light in her eye. It brought back a memory, barely noticed at the time.

'When the tmeg was pushing you over the cliff, we had an earthquake.' She crept on, rubbing her arm, frowning.

'They're coming more often aren't they?'

'Mmm. The ground opened up underneath me. It almost got me. I still tried to distract it, threw dirt in its eye.' She clenched her fingers.

'You did? I noticed a half-open eye. You shouldn't have put yourself in danger for me.'

'What are friends for?' She grinned, clambering over a ridge.

'Well, thanks. My dad's no help as usual. Let's hope the quake is over.'

'Didn't you notice the aftershocks back there, when we were running? This won't be a good place to be if we have another.' Gulping, Fay looked up at the cave roof, shrouded in gloom.

15

'I know. We need a way out. Recognise any of this, Fay? Been here before?'

'Nope. Plus, we could both be in different cave systems.' She bit her lip.

'What lives down here?'

'Apart from bobears, that pink fungus, don't ask.' Fay shivered.

'Oh.'

She could almost see him tugging his ear, suddenly feeling very alone, like her.

The heavy mrug on her leg slid down, reminding her she was not.

'Aah!' She tripped over it, thrusting her hands out.

There was nothing to save her.

Rushing darkness gobbled her up.

5

⋮Fishy⋮

Warmed by the spring, Ky stepped up to the rock, reached out toward the bobear glow.

Something hissed. He snatched back his hand, moving on.

A worn path wound through the rock. He followed it.

The trickling, splashing sounds echoed around him, somehow soothing.

Fay's scream tore through his head.

'Fay? You alright?'

Ky stopped, listening for the slightest sound. His stomach twisted into knots. Don't ask, she'd said.

He didn't want the mrug, cruising high above outside in concerned circles, down here at risk either. Chewing his lip, he sent it off to hunt.

'Think so. Fell down a shaft or something. I'll have a nice show of bruises tomorrow.' Fay's strained voice sent a rush of relief down his back.

'Can you see?' How would he ever find her if not?

'Can you?'

'Pink and steamy here.' He swiped his forehead with a damp arm.

'Here too. Pretty.'

He smiled, sagging with relief. Fay's constant presence in his head gave him the strength to move on.

The tunnel wound down, branching into small caves. Some had ledges, holes, perhaps fire pits. Bigger ones held huge, hanging stalactites like chandeliers, lit by the glow.

'Ah!' He hit the floor. The disturbed colony of pombats chittered and flapped away, thousands of them.

'What is it? You okay?' Fay's voice clanged through his head.

'Loads of pombats.' Ky clambered to his feet.

'Oh no.' Fay whispered.

'Reckon I scared them all out.'

'Ew.'

'Yes, I know how you hate pombats.' He rolled his eyes.

'That and my lovely mrug just peed down my leg again.'

'Ha. Sure it wasn't you?' Biting a smile, Ky crept on, aware of a rumbling sound that grew around him. He felt his tired shoulders bunch, imagining an army of sleeping monsters.

'I've followed it down to the bottom.

19

Something's rumbling...'

'Mine's come to a dead end. I'll try to get out of here.' Even in his head, her voice shook.

'I'll go on, then.' Eager, Ky strode further into the dimness.

Finally the tunnel opened into a giant, cathedral cavern. The pink glow was not bright enough to show the height or width of the misty chamber. Thunder drowned him, bouncing off the walls from a river that cascaded into a midnight lake.

'It's a waterfall. Wow...'

Ky followed rough steps down toward the lake. Closer, he could see the dark water teeming with long fish that flashed silver and blue. Standing on the bank, the surface seethed with a thousand little eyes.

He became aware of a drifting, heavy perfume in the mist that dewed his face. At either side of the falls, a vine twisted like his curling hair, threaded with glinting golden leaves and silver trumpet flowers as big as his head. One tress of it drifted beside the cascade, dancing in the splashes. Something long and golden gleamed, like a beacon. That scent, its swaying, dazed him. Drooping, hypnotised, he felt himself falling...

'Ky? Where are you now?'

Jerking back to the present, Ky shook his head.

'Still there. I've spotted something odd. Just have to ...'

'Ky?'

Frowning, he hunted around for a stick. He felt slow, clumsy, knocking off some of the pink ear-shaped fungus that glowed behind the vine.

Ripping off some of the old roots that snaked up the rock, he attempted to plait them together. He waited to feel the zing of the vine's pain, but either it was dead or he was just numb.

Leaning out over the water, suddenly queasy, he hooked the dancing, dangling frond towards him.

21

Carefully, he pinched the long golden pod away from the stem. Now surely, he would feel something...

'Wow!' He twirled it in his fingers, dazzled by its shine, its patterns that seemed to shift in the light. His head swam, full of tinkling melody. Was he imagining that high-pitched whine? Had those pink ears really swivelled towards him?

'Wow what?' Fay sounded peeved.

He jumped when something touched his foot. Looking down, Ky saw a long eel rising up like a snake from a slimy carpet of them around him. Although it had little eyes, its lumpy head was crocodile long.

It sank its teeth into his sandal strap.

Another slithered around his ankle, tightening.

'Aaah!' Leaping back toward the path, he shook them free, more eels snapping around his feet. Sliding, he stomped a few on the way. Their hisses grew louder, angrier. He shoved his prize in a pocket of his soft tunic.

22

'Ky! What is it?'

'Eels, fish, I dunno. Big heads; teeth. Coming out the pool after me.'

He backed away, still feeling sick. His head spun. Strange music rattled in his brain.

'Climb! Fish can't climb, can they?'

'I don't know if I can. Maybe it's the plants. I don't feel right...' He shook his head again, pinched his nose.

'There's a funny smell here too. It could be something growing in the cave.' Fay sounded a little dreamy.

Hopping back to the stone path, he glanced back. Eels came boiling out the water. In a wriggling river, their eyes gleamed in the rosy light.

He chanced a peek up into the darkness. The cavern walls reared up like cliffs.

Looking back, they'd formed a semi-circle around him. Organised predators, what else?

His only escape was up.

6

¦Ears¦

Fay, turning around from her second dead-end, tiptoed back along the tunnel, hands over her head.

'No pombats. No crawlies. I'm not in a cave, it's just dark,' she chanted, creeping along, eyes constantly darting toward the shadowed nooks. A host of ghost echoes whispered.

Something tickled her fingers as she

flexed them.

'Aah!' Her yelp rang off the walls, repeating into the distance.

She danced, flapping in a mad, silent whirl, huffing like a runner. Heart slamming, bumping off the boulders, she took off.

'Ky? I'm lost.' Her weary legs halted. Bent over, she gasped, holding her knees, listening.

The pale little mrug squeezed her damp leg. Maybe it was reassurance. Maybe it was a warning.

'Huh. That makes huh, two of us.' He sounded grim. *'Can we ping home now?'*

'I wish.' She sighed, glad to hear him inside her head.

'But I saw the beast go. We're okay.' Ky wheedled.

'What if you didn't see it come back?' She rolled her eyes at his glum silence.

Eventually, her heart slowed. She could breathe again.

Moving on, her sandals ground loud with every step. Her shadow seemed to leap around her.

Usually, she dreamed catastrophe. She hadn't dreamed this.

The rampant pink fungus on the walls looked like a million listening ears, eager for disaster.

The further she went, the darker it seemed, despite the rosy illumination.

Something scraped.

She stopped, quivering.

'Oh, for light, for a blimworm!' Her whisper rushed back at her like a thousand phantoms.

Breathless, she realised that the rushing wasn't just an echo.

Once her ghosts fell silent, the muted rumble came clear. Water. Maybe it was Ky's waterfall.

Her quick foot crunched loud, making her jump.

Looking down, dry-mouthed, she made out the remains of an egg, long abandoned. With her foot inside, it curled up toward her ankle like some fantastic shoe. A slinker egg.

The mrug's scarlet eyes met hers from her other leg.

She bent to check her skin, sighing her relief. There were no cuts on her leg. Any blood would attract all the crawlies.

She cast her mind out, searching.

The slinkers were close, asleep for now.

'Ky there're slinkers in here.'

He didn't reply.

Frowning, she quietly kicked off the shattered shell. It rolled, clonking between the stalagmites, out of sight. Wincing, she tiptoed toward the rumbling.

Like pink chandeliers, stalactites hung, feathered with growth. Their eternal drip was lost in a drone of sound.

She wove between them.

The sound grew with every step until she reached a rocky ledge that seemed to bar the way.

Beyond it, the water grumbled like a sleeping monster in the misty void. The ground shook with its power. Its breath

27

created a breeze that swirled the mist.

'I'm at another dead end, Ky. It ends in a kind of window.'

There was no answer. The ground shook harder, making her stagger.

'Ky?' She sucked her lip, staring up at the fangs trembling above. A drip struck cold on her cheek.

The only thing worse than being down here, was being down here alone.

7

⋮Up⋮

He turned, groping for a hand-hold. The eels' wet slithering turned into a rush behind him. He grabbed a gnarled vine with one hand, a ledge with another, hoisting himself up.

Don't think about the bugs. One foot braced on a rock, he pushed up again as jaws snapped beneath him.

The cliff shook.

His foot slipped, smearing pink fungus.

He dangled in the dark, panting, feeling sick.

Fangs grazed his sandal sole. He reached up to the vine again.

Something scuttled over his hand.

'Aah!' Snatching away, he swung out into space. His arm and fingers burned, holding on.

Teeth snapped around his flailing feet.

'Ky! I hear you close! What is it?'

'I'm climbing up.' Gritting his teeth, Ky reached out again into the dangerous dark.

Hand over shaking hand, feet jammed in crevices, sliding off rock, he scrambled up. Head spinning, he scraped his chest, knocked his elbows.

It was too dark to see whether these snaky fish could climb.

He banged his knees. The wall went up forever.

'I hear you coming, Ky. My dead end must lead into your cavern. Can you see me?'

'I don't know if they're following.' Ky

looked up. A pale blob danced before his eyes. '*Is that you?*'

He clambered faster.

'*I thought I'd lost you.*' Grabbing the back of his tunic, she ground him over the rocky lip into the tunnel. Wiping an arm across his sweaty forehead, he flopped, gasping on the floor.

'*Can you see them?*' He felt her presence move away, trying to control his heaving ribs.

'*Nope.*'

'*That doesn't mean they're not there, or coming.*' He groaned.

'*I know. Just get your wind back.*' She patted his shoulder.

Rubbing his sore chest, he strained his ears for any sound. No hope. The rush of the waterfall drowned everything. Yet still that tinkling song filled his head.

'Whew!' Finally his thundering heart began to slow down. He could speak again.

'*Shh! You'll wake the slinkers.*'

His head felt better.

31

'There must've been something in the perfume from those silver flowers...'

'Silver flowers?'

He focused on Fay's face looming above him. She was frowning.

'Yeah. Long trumpets. Gold leaves. Or at least they looked that way in the pink glow.' He shrugged.

'Oh!' Fay's eyes popped open, the whites bright in the gloom.

'What-?' He stopped as a rock clicked, tilting in the window to the cavern.

'Time to go.' Fay yanked him to his feet, leading him back through the rosy tunnels, one arm over her head.

'It must be safe to ping now.' Puffing, Ky tugged his ear, urging his shaky legs to carry him further.

'Not if it's still around. Or the eels.' Fay jogged on.

'Eels too?' Ky, tripped, recovered.

'Yup. Lots of possibles.'

'Great.'

The cold breeze drifting inside cooled Ky's still-wet clothes. His teeth chattered.

Staring only at Fay's bobbing ribbons, he followed like a zombie, jogging one foot in front of the other.

The air chilled as time went on. His whole body shook to the strange music in his head.

'Stop! We're outside!' Fay caught his arm, halting in the mouth of the cave.

Blinking, Ky looked up at the moon through the overhanging trees. A dark silhouette soared through the air high above. He gulped.

'My phone. I lost it back at the river.' Ky patted his pockets. The still-tinkling seed pod had taken its place.

'Are you mad? Haven't you seen enough?' Fay glared. 'It'll be alright until tomorrow. It doesn't even work.'

'I still need to fix it. Please. We can be real quick.'

'Remember your words.' She rolled her eyes.

33

'You sound just like my Mum.' A pang of loss ripped through him. He'd made his choice.

Fay sniffed, tapping her foot.

'Oh, yeah, toenail.' He grinned. 'Pleeease.'

'It's tonay for please, Ky. Oh rats.' Fay flipped her hands. 'I must be insane.'

'Let's go. Two pings, simple.' He sagged, grinning.

The rosy cave mouth faded before his eyes as they pinged.

What would he do if the beasts were waiting for them by the stream?

8

⋮Fry⋮

The new clinic felt like home now, since the ancient temple had crumbled. As ever, Ancients, faded to wise green lights, mingled with Elders in various stages of fading and shrinking with age on that journey. They joined with younger healers on an equal footing here, for the benefit of all.

Stretching, Fay left her private chamber

off the main tunnel, trotting down to the 'consulting rooms', a system of small pockets in the rock lit by blimworms. Breakfast already felt a long time ago.

Myn, Fay's first patient of the day, wrapped her arms tight around Fay, shuddering with pain.

Closing her eyes, Fay focused all her power into the body in her lap. She slid bones and tendons back into place, knitted skin back together.

'It's OK Myn. You're all fixed.' She stroked the scrubby head until the sobbing ceased. Likewise, her little mrug clung tight to her leg. Between them, it was like wearing a straightjacket. She could feel the baby mrug in her head, watching, wondering.

Finally, the girl looked up with huge, waterfall eyes.

'It doesn't hurt any more...' A sunrise smile broke across her face.

Fay stared at her, suddenly shaking as dreams engulfed her. She saw a cloud, raining blood, a field of bones. She saw this child screaming in terror.

'Fay?' Myn tipped her head, jiggling on her lap.

'Sorry.' Fay gulped, shaking her head, snapping back to the present. 'Take care now eh?'

This was the second time her dreams had come in the day. There must be some message there.

She watched the girl skip away, chewing her cheek.

⋮

'Ma got me a baby kittle!' Myn ran over to her table that night, carrying a ball of lilac fluff.

'A baby kittle's called a kitt, Myn.' Fay scratched her ear. 'Are you prepared for the hard work, replacing its mother?'

There was something about a kitt. You just had to reach out to touch that fluff.

'Replacing?' Myn frowned.

One flappy ear swung out as its tufty little head swivelled and dipped like a heavy bud on a stem. One fried egg eye looked out the front of its head, and one stared out the back. Between, the ears flapped with the nose slit beneath. Square teeth filled a mouth that circled the bottom of its head, working in segments.

'We only have kitts because their silly mothers will still hang upside down. Sometimes the extra weight of the baby is too much, so they fall. It's all that fluff that saves the babies.' Fay touched its softness, smiling.

One huge eye focused on her scratching finger, the other staring at the crowded benches behind.

'So I'm its Ma now.' Myn grinned, squeezing it tighter.

The long, fluffy tail wove in the air like a frightened snake.

'Gently, Myn. What have you called it?' Fay laughed as the long, flat tongue swiped a stripe across her hand.

'I thought I'd call it Fay, after you.'

Fay stared at her, grimacing. Kittles were so stupid, so unpredictable.

'I'd rather you call it Fry. It's close but not too close.' She watched the temptation to object fade in those limpid eyes.

'Sounds like we're going to cook it.' Myn sniggered. 'Okay. C'mon Fry. Let's introduce you.' She ran off.

Bobbing, the kitt stared back over her shoulder, or maybe it looked ahead.

'That was sweet.' Fyl, her friend, smiled, wiping his bobonut shell clean with the heel of his loaf. 'She's a fan.'

'That kitt's going to be a menace with her in charge of it.' She shook her head.

'At least you'll probably never see it again.'

'Hope not.' Fay continued with her dinner, finding fragments to tempt her mrug.

'I think it's great that you have a mrug.' Fyl pointed at it, watching the huge scarlet eyes fixed on Fay.

'You know all about them, with the

breeding ponds on your farm. Can I ask your advice sometimes?'

''Course.' He shrugged.

'Just hope I can bring it up to be useful. I'm under pressure to get it right.' She grimaced.

'You will. You may be the first girl to ever have one, but I'll see you're okay. Ky seems to be doing alright with his.'

'Does he? It doesn't always come when he calls.' Fay fed hers another morsel.

'Ha. Nor does mine. They have minds of their own.' Fyl shrugged. 'You have to accept that. It's not always convenient.'

'It's not convenient when they wet all down your leg, either.' Fay grimaced, peeling the mrug's miniature, manta-ray wings off and setting it down. She flapped the sopping fabric of her trouser leg. 'Ew.'

'It'll find a way to tell you soon. You have to pay attention, it may be subtle.' Fyl laughed.

'I don't know if subtle is quite the word.'

She wrinkled her nose.

'Ha. You, with all your dreams of the future that could happen any time! It's just the same. You have to wait to see.'

'That's what I was afraid of.' Fay thrust her fists into her pockets, staring into the sunset.

9

⋮Unfair⋮

Ky's eyelids flickered, lifted and closed. He snuggled back under the blankets, eager to return to his dream of riding the mrug, not the nightmare of rolling in the log. The endless flyer squawks continued outside, drilling into his head. The scent of the forest filtered in. A song drifted on the wind from the valley below. Power sizzled in the air.

'It's a work day.' Sitting up, he rubbed his

eyes.

Squinting in the glare sneaking around the edge of the shutter, he spotted his phone on the shelf. Remembering that huge eye, those claws, the eels, he shuddered.

'Must be late.'

It wasn't that he'd be in trouble. This wasn't Earth where he never got anything right. It just made him feel guilty when everyone else seemed to work non-stop. They were getting the job done with food and sleep at a minimum. Rebuilding half a planet was a mammoth task.

'They must take a rest some time.' Yawning, he knuckled his eyes again.

He slid into yesterday's soft trousers and tunic. Faint music tinkled through his head.

Scratching, he opened the door, strolling out into the cool morning. On the stump, a breakfast shell and juice had been left for him, covered with a leaf. He should have been up to go fetch it.

'Fay? Thanks for breakfast.'

'You're such a snoozer! I've been working for hours!'

Stretching, he squinted into watery sunlight. It bounced, blinding, off thousands of wet surfaces.

'I was dreaming of riding my mrug.' He grinned.

Shielding his eyes, he gazed across the valley to the hazy mountains in the distance. His cruising mrug made a diamond silhouette close by. One day he'd be up there too.

He smiled at the warm glow of its greeting, calling it down.

His grandparents had chosen this special spot. It would be beautiful again once the scars of the devastation had healed.

The site of the new village lay far below, stretching up the opposite slope, each house making use of the surviving trees for support and privacy.

He stepped back, in case he was spotted, an old habit from earth school. Maybe they hadn't noticed his absence yet.

The mrug landed beside him, waving happy corners. He frowned. It wasn't usually so excited. His dream flooded back.

'Is today the day?' Ky stared down at it, feeling his stomach flip. It sent back a warm glow.

'You know how long I've waited for this.' He licked his lips.

Crouching down, he set a hand on one of the tentacles that dangled behind its eyes. It was warm, smooth. The mrug didn't object.

'Ready?' His heart thumped.

Kneeling, Ky wrapped his fingers tight around the tendril, reaching forward for the second. Slowly, he slid a leg onto the wing. Scarlet eyes flashed up at him. Pain screamed through his head.

The mrug shot up into the sky. Dragged up with it, Ky's shocked fingers locked tight around the tendrils.

'Sorryyyy!' Legs thrashing, he dangled as the creature spun. It crashed through the branches of a tree. Battered, he clung on, panting.

The world swirled around him as the mrug dived between the forest trunks. It swooped and spun. Twigs lashed his face. Reflexively, his fingers tightened. Another branch caught him in the ribs.

'Owww!' This wasn't the kind of flying he'd dreamed.

Finally it plunged into the stream, dumping him on his face. At last his fingers released. The mrug zipped away, broadcasting fright and pain.

Shaking, Ky coughed his way back to the cabin. He hung his wet clothes over a bush, inspecting the damage. Scratched and bruised, he was lucky. Even if his face stung.

So much for his dreams, he thought, glum. Climbing into his last clothes, he broadcast regret, hoping the mrug would forgive him.

Returning outside, it was nowhere in sight.

Lying back in soft grass, nursing his

throbbing rib, he wound up his power, locating a suitable log from the stash in the next valley where he'd set them ready.

He floated it over the hill and down to the site below, adding it to their depleted pile.

Hunger drove him to rise, stiff and sore, to take up his breakfast after just five more.

'Dad?' Too late now, but it would be good to know he was still there somewhere.

'Ky. Something wrong?'

'Not now. Yesterday there was. You didn't answer me.' Ky ground a particularly hard nut between his teeth.

'I was in a long meeting with the Ancients yesterday. The change in orbit has given us a lot of problems with more still emerging. What happened yesterday?'

'A monster almost got me. Fay said it was a tmeg.' Ky shuddered, rubbing his rib.

'Why didn't you ping away?'

'Fay said not to...' Ky felt his ears burn.

'Ha. Better to try than get eaten, I'd have thought.'

Ky ground another hard nut to powder.

'Well you're talking to me, so I guess there's nothing to worry about.'

'I needed you Dad! You weren't there when I called.' Ky found it suddenly hard to swallow. *'You're never there any more...'*

'Here you're a man now, Ky. You can't keep calling me for every little thing. I have a responsibility to the Ancients, to the planet.'

'Little thing! I could have died!' Ky shook with rage. *'You're my dad. Mum's partner. Doesn't that mean something?'* He kicked a stone.

'Look. I can't do this now. I have another meeting. We'll get together soon, okay?'

The connection broke.

'Yahhh!' Yelling, Ky lobbed his empty shell into the valley, wiping his wet face on his sleeve. 'He never even said sorry!'

He limped up and down the path, kicking pebbles over the cliff. Breakfast sat like concrete in his stomach. He wished he could start the day over again.

His mrug floated down, circling around him. Ignoring it, he stopped, glaring out at the valley. Something moved between the trees. He stared, feeling the muscles bunch in his neck. He caught a glimpse of long, dangling umbo scales, that droopy, groping nose and flappy ears. His held breath whooshed out.

The mrug settled by his feet. Slowly, the soothing glow from it worked its magic. It must have forgiven him. Stroking it, he didn't make the mistake of trying to get on its back again.

Sighing, Ky reached out to pull yesterday's prize from his pocket, aware of that music still chiming in his head. It had a rhythm to it, like breathing. Perhaps it was coming from this.

Twirling it in his fingers, he was mesmerised. It shone bright gold with delicate traceries that shifted on its surface like something alive. Longer than his hand, thicker than his thumb, it had to be magic.

He recalled Fay's eyes popping in the

49

cave, just before they had to run. She knew, just from his description. But oh, how she liked her secrets too.

Maybe there just wasn't time to tell him.

Like Dad never had time for him either.

Perhaps he'd just hide it for a while to see what she'd do. That would even things up.

Smiling, he went inside, tucking it into the secret pocket of his old waistcoat at the bottom of his chest. Locking it, he hid the key under a rock in the corner. He didn't need to wear that old thing any more. He was used to the soft tunic and wide trousers that everyone else wore. He became more Mraxi every day.

'Better get down to proving it with hard work.' He stood up, rolling up his sleeves.

⋮

Ky couldn't wait for dinner, so they could talk.

'That monster yesterday, it was a tmeg?'

'Tmeg.' Fay nodded, nibbling her berry bread.

'It trapped me in that log. I got a much-too-close look of this big, orange eye, and the long claws when it started to smash it up. Then it tipped me out into the lake. It was using its claws and tail to hold on as it climbed down that cliff.' Ky shuddered. 'It was flapping its wings for balance. I expected it to swoop down on me any second.'

'Yup. Typical tmeg.' Shrugging, Fay sat back on her rock, chewing.

She dug out a berry, throwing it up.

'Ah, the only thing I miss about Earth school.' Ky caught it in his mouth.

'Mmm. We were right to run.'

'For sure.' Ky snorted as juice flooded his mouth. 'Why couldn't we ping away?'

'They can't do it themselves but sometimes creatures have managed to piggyback with someone and a few killed them on arrival. We're not sure how. It pays to be careful.'

'That I believe.' He popped out another berry, tossing it up for her to catch. She snapped it from the air, laughing.

'Ha! 'S not the same when it's not chocolate.' She pulled a face.

'Ah, how I miss chocolate.' He licked his lip.

'Me too.' Fay sighed. 'You ache. Want me to-?' She wiggled her fingers.

'I'm fine. Had you been in those caves before?' He rubbed his sore rib.

'Nope. Pombats, all those creepies...' Fay shuddered, shaking her ribbons. 'But I dreamed we'd go there, knew we'd find our way out.'

He knew she dreamed what would happen but never when or how. She kept a lot of secrets, for everyone's peace of mind, she said.

'Thanks for sharing.' He ground another mouthful, hard.

'Ky, you know how it is!' She slapped her knee. 'I shared before and it didn't help, did it?'

'Unfair, is how it is.' He crunched the final nut, hopping down. 'Would've been nice to know we'd get out alright.'

'If I tell you that, maybe we won't!'

'La, la, la, la.' Ky covered his ears.

Fay tugged his hands down.

'You might feel you could slow down, or sit down to rest and that would change everything!' Fay jerked his hands, eyes fierce.

'I've heard it a thousand times. It still bugs me.' Yanking away, he went to wash his hands in the stream.

'Well, deal with it. I can't help my dreams.' She sniffed, standing up. 'If you're gonna be grumpy, I'm off.'

'Wait! Did you find out about the eels?' Ky turned back, flapping his hands dry.

'Wouldn't you like to know.' She grinned and tossing her hair, vanished.

10

⋮Wish⋮

Fay had put off the inevitable as long as she could, nodding in her seat by the fire. Her exhausted body wouldn't let her stay awake. Dropping onto her bed, still half-way through her usual wish for a dreamless night, she blinked off like a light.

Immediately, she found herself on a sultry plain in the shadow of a dark cloud.

Maybe it was a storm brewing. She didn't have her usual storm headache yet. She gazed at her surroundings, trying to find something familiar. Crumbled desert with its garnish of thorny growths and rubbery ear-plants stretched away flat in all directions, the sandy soil in swathes of mis-matched colours. Jagged rock hills surrounded the plain and something she couldn't make out flickered in that distant haze. One cliff in particular felt familiar.

Something screamed. Usually her dreams were silent.

Shock shivered down her spine. She'd never get used to the sound of pain. Her stomach clenched. She couldn't tell if she were awake or dreaming.

Jerking her head around, she saw that the darkest corner of the cloud was leaking fat drops of dark rain. Beneath it, a wild kittle danced, demented. Its screams cut through her like knives.

She turned towards it, hesitating as it

staggered nearer. No longer was this the bouncing prance of a kittle. It wobbled, tripping. Now she could see the lavender fur smoking, singed clumps falling off.

By the time it reached her, its poor face was a twisted, melting mess.

It dashed past her, plunging down a dip.

She leapt after it, feeling sick. The poor beast was trying to ease its burning skin with desperate rolling in the cool sand.

Another jumped on top of it, howling. Driven mad by the pain, they began to bat at one another, bud heads bobbing on their seared stalks.

The shrieks rose higher, to be joined by others behind.

Whipping round, she found a stampede of howling creatures, bloody, burnt, leaping straight at her...

She jerked awake, sweating. Her cave was still dark. Someone was pounding on her door. She had a flap, not a door. It was just her heart slamming in her chest. Wasn't it?

She lay there, rigid, haunted by their tortured eyes, ears still ringing with their pain. It felt like the end of the world.

Fumbling stiffly for her blimworm, she hooked it up, to chase away the dream and the dark.

Seeing the bare cave walls, her meagre collection of belongings and the blanket from home on her bed, she felt the tension start to drain away.

Her pulse began to slow. She swiped an arm across her damp forehead.

When she was little, waking from such dreams, her parents would have rushed into the room, alarmed at the terror she would broadcast.

To their relief, over the years she'd learned to block the emotions generated from her dreams until she was properly awake.

So now, no-one knew what she suffered each night. No-one came running to comfort her.

She sobbed alone.

Her new routine was to check on the family and friends in her head. She would know who was sleeping, who was awake. She would know if they were alright. Then she would write the dream in her book for future reference, clear its shadow from her mind.

This routine gave her new focus, calmed her so she could get ready to begin her new day.

Fay put the book away, stretched and sat up. She took a deep breath.

'Ugh!' Gagging, she bounced out of bed.

'Ew.'

The little mrug smiled up at her, smearing poo.

'I should have found you a nappy.'

Dragging on her clothes, she stripped the sticky blankets, dropping them in the clinic laundry.

Someone was in for a nasty surprise but she had no way to do it herself.

She washed and rinsed the mrug at the fountain, holding it out to drip away from her body.

Shuddering, she worked hard to stifle the screaming ghosts that still echoed in her brain from the dream. It clung somehow, despite writing it down.

She gritted her teeth.

'It's not the last nightmare I'll have and it might not happen for years.'

Her muttered words gave her no comfort at all.

⋮

'Don't look at me like that. Pananas. Hello. I knocked earlier. You know how it is, I can't tell you everything.' Voyn shrugged, waiting outside the door flap, making her jump as she left for work.

'Don't I just, Pa. You're early. Must be important.' She switched from one anxious foot to the other, tugging her bows.

'Outside.' He beckoned, heading out.

Fay sighed, every howl and keen still ringing in her head.

'Two things. First, since we changed the orbit, the crust plates are moving. The Sour Sea is at risk, even the Tower. We are expecting many earthquakes.' He scowled. 'Mudslides, landslips, you know.'

'No injuries?'

'None, so far. A team are watching. You will be the first to know, of course. Say nothing for now but be prepared. This is uncharted territory. It seems to be getting worse. Scour your dreams Fay. You are the only one who can see forward. The entire planet could be at risk.' He waved a wild arm, tugged his hair.

'Great.' She narrowed her eyes. 'Alright. You said two things?'

'The Ancient, Luna had a vision. She's predicting black rain, mauve snow, eclipses of the sun and death. '

'Has she gone mad? Death?' Fay grimaced, shaking inside. 'Mauve snow?'

'There's no guarantee this would all happen at once. Have you dreamed any of those things?'

'I don't think so. I'll check the books.' She frowned.

'The problem is, Boyng is forecasting the eclipses start imminently.'

'That soon?' Fay stared up at her Pa.

He nodded.

'The clock's tock ticking, as they say.'

⁝

'Ky?' Fay sighed, fighting a stab of envy for his hide-away cabin with the panoramic view. Compared to her bare, dark cave, it was paradise.

Swirling wraiths of mist danced between the trees in the valley.

The first timbers were beginning to float around the skeleton buildings below, although she couldn't see any people among the ancient trees.

Behind her, a warbling chorus of squirts welcomed the day.

Rainbow flyers zipped past, vanishing

into the trees behind her.

An eagle keened high overhead.

She set the breakfast shell and mug on the stump outside his cabin, trying to decide what she was supposed to tell him.

There was no reply to her call.

She wandered to the stream that chuckled across the clearing to plunge over the cliff. Where it widened into a pool, she caught sight of her reflection. Falling to her knees, she gasped. One side of her head, the curls she'd fought to tame last night were gone. Beneath her bow, her hair fell straight as heavy rain.

She wrapped it around one hand squeezing it tight. It unrolled, a smooth ribbon of silk, far longer than the other side, without a kink.

She scowled. Something was wrong, even if it meant half the battles with the brush.

Rolling her eyes at the closed door flap, tugging her rope of hair, she pinged away.

11

⁞Smashed⁞

'Ky! Could you lend a hand a minute?' Someone called up from the valley. He'd made sure a good pile of timber awaited them this morning.

Ky set aside his phone, feeling guilty that Fay had again brought him breakfast.

His mrug was splashing in the stream. It could find him soon enough from the air, if it needed to.

Blinking, he turned toward the sound, pinging down.

'What can I do?' All he could make out was a man's silhouette, perched high on the log frame. A shining, bark-less tree trunk dangled below him, set on knotted guide ropes.

'Touch that end into the hole for me, would you?' An arm and finger pointed.

Leaning his whole weight on it, puffing, Ky heaved it into the notch. It slipped in with a satisfying thump.

'Good. Thanks Ky.' The man slid down off the pole with a thud. He recognised Bryn by his distinctive plait as he trotted away.

All around him power crackled in the air, where the carpenters worked the wood. The scent of cut timber filled his nostrils. Several beams swung in mid-air around him.

'Watch out! Hey. Can you shove that one for me?' Tem called as Ky ducked.

'Hi Tem. Haven't seen you for a while.' Ky waved.

Grinning, he hurried towards it, glad to help. It delayed another scavenging trip to the ruined valley for materials a little longer. Alone there, he felt exposed as he salvaged, sorted and piled the debris. He was always glad when one of the others came to help. The job was far better once he could pick from his heaps, safely back at the cabin.

As he grasped the next log, he felt a tremor in the ground. It vibrated up his leg, through his body, rattled his teeth.

'Tmeg alert!'

'Take cover!'

The shouts echoed off the walls, bounced around his brain. Cold sweat suddenly drenched him. He froze. The beam dropped to the ground, just missing his foot.

Men were sliding down the poles, running. Looking back he made out a familiar row of jagged spikes moving behind the trees.

Tem grabbed his arm, pulled him along with the crowd. Stumbling, he fled down into a cave just in time for the circular stone door to be rolled across the entrance.

Shaking, all Ky could see was that orange eye at the end of the hollow log, those claws clinging on the cliff, sunset scales, drooling fangs.

'Fay?' Casting out, he could feel her concentration. She must be working.

The ground shook harder. In the silence, a muffled roar snuck around the door. Straining, Ky became aware again of the music tinkling in his head. Then he heard the faint smash of splintering wood. A muttering started up in the crowd, drowned by another crash, then more.

Eventually, there was silence. Light rose from several blimworms.

Still, they waited.

Ky hunkered into a corner, in no hurry to go outside again. He consoled himself that he was with a whole group that felt exactly the same.

Something scuttled over his foot. Peering

down in the shadows he glimpsed legs and a long, curling stinger poised above.

'Scorpion!' he yelled, jumping away.

'What's that?' Puzzled glances zeroed in on him.

'It's like a big spider er webber, with stingers over the top. I didn't think they were here.' Ky shuddered, peering down.

'Oh. A stabwebber.' Everyone gasped, instantly shuffling away. 'Where?'

Tem approached, waving his light in his hand.

'Here somewhere.' Ky pointed around his feet.' It's gone. It crawled over my foot.'

'Crawled? Ha.' Tem grinned.

He looked up, startled, as everyone began to laugh.

'What's funny?' He scowled.

'Stabwebbers make a web big enough for a man. That must have been a hatchling. No danger yet. Still it was good that you warned us.' Tem patted him on the shoulder.

Ky was glad of the dark to hide his

burning face.

Eventually, the stone circle was rolled away. One cautious scout stepped outside.

Beckoning the others, they moved off to check the damage.

'My mrug!' Ky pinged back home.

Materialising up the silent hill, he rocked on his feet, lungs flat with shock.

The timbers of Jax and Dit's wooden home were smashed. The lumpy mingo tree that supported one corner leaned out over the cliff. The young, red-leaved tree on the opposite corner had been snapped clean off. An explosion of chunks and splinters filled the inside, spreading outward.

The furniture looked as if it had been flung about in rage. Grandad Jax would not be pleased.

The blood froze in his veins. Maybe it was still there. His stomach flip-flopped. Vision telescoping he scanned for the tmeg. It made his head swim.

The mrug dropped over his head. He

staggered, blinded as the creature massaged his scalp. Warmth and comfort spread through him.

'Gerroff. I need to see!' He peeled it off, spinning it into the wind. Shaking, his eyes darted between the trees.

Jumping, he looked up as flyers began squawking again.

Nearby, his precious chest had been kicked through a bush, still locked. He dug the key out from the corner, buried under wreckage.

'Well I've never seen anything like that before.' Bryn made his heart stop, pinging in beside him. He scratched his head. 'Such bad luck. Why would it pick on you?'

'How often do they come near people?' Ky husked, wondering if it remembered him.

'Hardly ever. Good thing we have fall-back plans, just in case, like the cave.' He frowned down at Ky.

'Has it gone?' Ky flicked haunted eyes to the trees. At least he wasn't alone.

'The flyers are singing. We're okay.' Bryn shrugged.

'Where will I sleep now?' Ky bit his lip, staring at the damage, digging out his cracked phone. Ha. He'd probably never sleep again.

'With your help, we'll have it all fixed by tonight, no problem.' Materialising beside them, Tem inspected some of the shattered wood, fingers already working out the repairs. 'You might want to pick up all your things, though...'

Ky set to work, fast.

The tmeg would be back.

12

⫶Smells⫶

Healers assembled under the dome of the largest cave in the clinic. The flitter screamed, writhing, blood spurting as its hearts pumped it out. An acrid scent filled the room. Helpers tried to rope its six lethal legs and the Ancients, now just green light, attempted to calm.

Fay's team of healers were struggling.

She ducked as its flailing tail whipped over her head.

'Fight with a tmeg.' Eryl the eldest healer, nodded, dark eyes sad.

A wing spar smashed down beside her, jetting a shower of gravel floor.

'It's really hard to concentrate,' Fay muttered, jumping as one junior healer got in the way of the claws, shrieking.

Thrashing, the beast clawed at the walls, flapping their supplies to the floor.

At last, the Ancients, glowing green at the shoulder of every Elder, gained control of it.

Gradually, it sank to the floor.

The relieved healers drew close, setting their hands on its glossy midnight scales.

Around them, another team scuttled in, tying more ropes to heavy rings in the walls, looping around those barbed legs, just in case it woke up.

Unnoticed, a second team ushered the injured people to another cave for healing.

Finally, Fay surfaced, satisfied at last that

the slashes were mended, the bones repaired.

Inside this huge cavern she had no way to gauge the time of day. She felt like an age had passed.

Power swirling cold, the healed flitter vanished, released back to its lair. Everyone sighed.

Drained and starving, she plodded out to the Healer's room with the team to wash and restock with bread and juice. It took a long time to regain the energy to even talk.

⋮

Eventually, with no further patients, she set off for the supplies room. Inside, Fyl was glum, knotting precious ropes and ticking lines on a slate.

'Pananas! Hello! Cool hair.' He grinned, flushing. 'Will the flitter live?'

She settled down to help sliding his comment into the darkest corner of her head. She didn't need any more worries right now.

Maybe practice would make her better at

this. Everyone took a turn when they could. On Mrax there was no longer such a thing as spare time, nor boredom.

'I think so. He'll need to rest for a while.' She sank back onto her seat.

'So you let him go?' He ticked his slate.

'Had to. We don't have anywhere to keep him. Especially since he snapped all his ropes. Sorry. I could see a good cave in his head. That's where we sent him. At least his wings were okay.'

'Good. Wish I could do what you do.' Fyl shoved another pile of ropes across the table, sending her neat pile cascading. 'It must have been better going to school on Earth, than doing this!' He flung a coil across the room.

'Ha. School there was a real pain. Hardly any practical stuff at all. No Legends. All books and computers. No wonder they're so behind.' She shook her head, retrieving the tangle from the corner.

'Don't they have Elders and Ancients?' He sat, throwing down his slate with a clatter.

'They have grandparents, but often no-one listens to them. Being old there is not always a good thing. Elders' wisdom is rarely appreciated.'

'I wouldn't know anything without my folks.' Fyl disappeared behind the table, came up with another snapped rope. 'Gah!'

'It's different if your folks teach you. That's our way. Everything passed down from the older generation. I've been wondering lately if that's a bit limited too...' Fay frowned.

'Balzar didn't teach Ky much at all. He didn't fit in on Earth either. Like me.' Fay sighed, remembering. 'It seems to have expanded his thinking somehow...'

'How do you mean?' He frowned

'He's different. Unpredictable. Dangerous.' Fay shivered. 'You know about my dreams. I have so many about him. They all end badly...' She sank back to her seat, twirling a curl around her finger. Her mrug squeezed her leg.

'But your dreams may be decades in the

future! I think somehow you just scroll through possible futures. Maybe he could change those futures...' Fyl's eyebrows rose.

'I just wish so many of them didn't come true...' She met his eyes. 'Even yours.'

'Mine? What do you mean?' He straightened.

'You had that fall last week.' She shrugged, tugging the bow in her curly hair.

'You saw that?' He probed his head, wincing.

'A while back, yes.' She nodded, testing her other bow, flicking the straight length of hair behind her shoulder.

'You're just full of secrets you can't tell, aren't you? Must be hard.' He frowned.

'I suppose I'm used to it by now.' She found herself blinking back tears. The whole planet was threatened but she couldn't tell. It all just festered inside. If only Ky could be so understanding.

A sudden warm sensation slid down her leg.

'Oh no!' Peeling off the little mrug she set it on the floor. Her trousers were soaked.

'You grew up with mrugs. Can you watch mine for a minute? I'll have to go change.' She shot off down the corridor.

Returning in clean trousers to the supplies room, she fixed the mrug back on her leg, gratified at the soft greeting she felt in her head.

'You let me know and I ignored it. I'm sorry.' She touched its pointed nose. 'I guess I'm the one who needs training.'

'All healers and helpers to heal zone three now, tonay, please. Umbo injury.'

'Oh dear, here we go again.' Fyl abandoned the ropes with a grin. 'You'll need all the help you can get.'

The umbo bellowed, piercing, the distinctive clatter of the plates on its back resounding up the corridor as it struggled. The heavy scent of marsh mud hung in the air.

Trotting out, Fay shared the poor umbo's

shrieking pain.

'Come on team, there's work to be done!' Rolling up her sleeves, she burst into the chamber echoing with the injured umbo's squeals.

13

⁝Bubble⁝

'Dad! I found you.' Ky stomped in as his father tugged on a sandal, sitting on his rumpled bed. Sunlight streamed in, windows wide to admit the morning flyersong.

'Ky! Pananas.' Balzar smiled.

Ky sagged with relief. Perhaps he was in a better mood.

'So this is what you've been up to! You're finished building?' Distracted, Ky turned a circle, taking in live trees and bubble glass. 'It's great.'

'All ready for Mum to visit.' Grinning, Balzar stood up, dropping his arm across his son's shoulders. 'Good to see you Ky.'

'You too.' Ky squeezed him back, blinking fast. 'Dad, I need to talk to you.' He took a deep breath, rubbing his chest.

'Sit.' Flapping a hand, Balzar poured them each some juice. His eyes were suddenly piercing below his dark brows.

'A tmeg smashed up the cabin.' Ky blurted, feeling his heart thud. 'I don't know if it was the same one that chased me before.'

'They do sometimes get a bit destructive, especially if they're frustrated. I wouldn't worry about it.' Balzar shrugged.

'It came to the new site. We had to shelter in the cave.' Ky muttered, swinging a foot. 'It was only my cabin. Nothing else. It was after me.'

'Ha! After you!' His father slapped his leg, slopping his drink.

'Let me explain-'

'Ky you're letting this place get to you. I know it's been a big adjustment.' Dad's eyes were dancing. 'Come see the view.'

'It's not that-' Ky chewed his cheek, slowly standing.

'You just need to give it some time, son. You imagine how freaked your Mum's gonna feel, if you're still having the jitters now.' Balzar opened the door, stepping onto the deck. Staring into the distance, he suddenly sobered.

'You never come when I call!' Ky bit out, tugging his hot ear as he stepped outside. 'You won't leave her alone too, will you?'

'The Ancients-' Balzar began, jutting his chin.

'Dad, I know you've been important to the Ancients for a long time.' Ky stared at the panorama below, sniffing perfumed wind. 'But you're not the only one. It would be good to know you're there for me, especially when I'm in a corner.' He fought to control his trembling lip.

'Ky-'

'You didn't even answer me!' Ky gulped, sucking his dry tongue. 'You won't do that to her, will you?'

'Of course not.' His father dipped his head, perhaps to avoid meeting his eyes.

'You'll regret it if you do.' He snarled. Dad still hadn't said sorry.

'She'll have you too, don't forget.' His father's narrowed eyes bored into his.

'Of course.' Ky looked away, angry heat scalding his face. It sounded like it was going to be up to him, for a change.

Opening his mouth to snap, he shut it again. Shouting wouldn't help him get Dad back, even if he felt like punching something.

'All this glass is tmeg proof, is it?' His eyes flicked to the bubble window with the panorama beyond.

'Absolutely. Designed for it.' Balzar grinned.

'When's she coming?' Ky couldn't resist a

little bounce.

'Soon. You'll be the first to know. Don't worry.'

Ky ground his teeth: That phrase again, 'don't worry.'

Did his dad know him at all?

14

⫶Spit⫶

With too much on her mind, Fay pinged to the shore, where the sea pounded in. The salt and spice wind that tugged her hair was full of the cries of seaflyers.

Beach dragging at her feet, the heavy mrug slid down, tripping her. She sprawled. Spitting sand, picking it from her curls, sliding it from her straight hair, she struggled to her knees.

'Ugh.' She wiped her face with her sleeve.

Wrapping the mrug higher, she moved on. Hopping over rocks with a pang of guilt, she picked up a pebble.

'Why tell me, Pa?!' Yelling, she flung it into the furious surf. 'Don't I have enough in my head?'

Concentrating hard on the next throw, she almost tripped over the gaut, tangled in ribbon-weed on the tideline.

Immediately, her memory began to chase through her nightmares, seeking references to a gaut.

Kneeling, she unwound the weed, touching the creature's smooth, domed forehead. She swept the drooping orange fringe away from its ring of closed eyes. With her other hand, she folded the lustrous cape and tender fins out the way. The heavy, scaled tail did not even twitch, yet she caught the faintest flicker of life.

Placing both hands on its smooth, muscled ribs, she closed her eyes. Warmth

85

burned through her, down into the ancient creature on the sand. Faintly it quivered. The round fish-eyes drifted open. It stared at her.

'I welcome death.' It whispered in her mind. That final word stretched into infinity, blowing through her head. *'I have lived long. Let me go.'*

'I can heal you!' Fay lied, wet warmth trickling down to her chin.

'We both know that is not true. Take my cape, you have one who needs it.' The orange feathering at its crown fluttered.

'I can't. It's part of you.' Fay shook her head, fighting back a sob.

'My spirit will go with it.' The long, trailing fins rose feebly to tug at the silvery cape attached to the narrow shoulders. *'Take it. It is our way.'*

The faltering fins had detached one part.

Biting her lip, Fay gave it a tug. The shimmering cape came free. It seemed to clasp her hands.

She felt sick.

'Now let me go. Have no regrets. It's my time.' The gaut's whisper tailed off.

The spark went out.

Fay fell to her knees. The delicate cape in her icy hands fluttered, settling to rest warm across her shoulders like a hug.

'But Mraxi can't die!' howled Fay into the streaming wind.

15

⁞Plop⁞

Ky's shoulders were stiffening as sunset approached. Maybe it was tiredness. More likely it was because he kept seeing the tmeg's long tongue with every shadowed stripe. Somehow its gaping maw was everywhere.

'Fay?'

'Ky, sorry. I'm tied up. See you at dinner.'
She slammed the window to her mind shut.

His grandparent's tiny cabin was remade,

full of the scent of fresh cut wood, reminding him with every breath. Even the mingo tree had been righted, though only the stump of the red-leaved tree remained to hold up the frame.

Sniffing, the mrug joined him inside, hovering by the rafters.

'Yes, every sniff tonight is going to remind me.' He eyed it, biting his lip. 'A ride on you would really make me feel better.'

He lifted his hand. The mrug came lower for a scratch.

'Can we try again?' Ky reached for a tentacle. The creature twitched away. Frowning, he rubbed his tender rib, remembering the last time.

Sighing, he stroked a hand over its ridged back. Big eyes flicking up to his face, it wriggled, broadcasting delight.

It had to be teasing him.

Stroking it again he reached towards its face corner. He hooked a gentle hand over the wing as it squirmed. His other hand hooked the other side.

Teeth gritted, he sprung onto its back.

Surprised, the mrug shot upwards.

'No!' His shoulders smashed against the new rafters. 'Ow!'

It swung round, clipping him on the rebuilt wall. Outrage seared his head.

Shooting stars exploded behind his eyes. He lost his grip.

'Aah!' He plunged to the hard floor, flattening Jax's hand-carved chair on the way.

All the air shot out of his lungs. He lay flopping, breathless as a fish out of water.

It seemed like hours before one desperate gasp let air in. Heaving ribs still sore from his last attempt, he panted away the dizzy feeling.

The mrug's red eyes glowed scarlet as it circled above.

He was never going to ride it, like this.

'Thanks a lot.' He grated through his aching throat and cavernous disappointment.

It floated outside with a sniff.

Lying there, dark memories crowded in with every sawdust gasp. His head throbbed.

Eventually, sore and grumpy, he stacked the remnants of Jax's chair and Dit's broken artwork by the wall. They would have to be mended another day.

Setting the bedding back on the mesh of twine he hauled in the rest of Jax's furniture. Finally, aching all over, he dragged in his heavy chest.

'Ha. Forgot to ping it.' He puffed, smacking his sweaty forehead.

Unlocking it, picking at splinters, he flipped back the lid. The eternal tinkling started up louder in his head. Frowning, he pulled the pod from its hiding place, marvelling at its mysterious, shifting pattern.

His fingers grazed the photo he'd tucked down the side. He pulled it out, staring down at his parents. It had been taken after he'd rescued Dad from the alien ship, after Mum's long spell in a coma.

Mum still looked so skinny after her accident, but her fingers meshed tight with Dad's. Thin also from his own ordeal, Dad was pulling a face. It was literally another world. Ky sank to the bed, rubbing his thumb across their faces. Life was so different here...

The mrug slapped down over his head. Its carpet of soft, wiggly legs massaged gently. He was enveloped in its salty smell. A mrug hug. It must have forgiven him and picked up how he was feeling.

'I didn't mean to-,'

'Surprise!'

Lifting a corner, Ky peeked out from beneath the mrug.

'Fay?'

'Ha! Your faces!' Fay laughed.

Cheeks burning, he peeled it off his head. Grumpy, it swooped away.

'Pananas.' Fay had pinged into the doorway, haloed by the fading sunset.

'Bananas.' Ky returned the greeting,

ramming the photo back, locked the lid shut.

'What happened?' Sniffing, she stepped inside, frowning.

'Nothing!' He shot a guilty glance at the mrug. 'Oh, a tmeg smashed this up for me. All Dit's lovely things are broken.' Ky folded his few clothes onto a shelf, wincing as his bruised shoulders stung. His stomach gurgled. The nuts and fruit at lunchtime seemed a lifetime ago.

'A tmeg did this? Looks good rebuilt. Why didn't you tell me?' She looked around. He noticed she looked pale and strained.

'I tried. We were busy. I thought you might have sensed it...' Alerted by a different waft, he sniffed his armpit, grimacing. 'I really should wash my clothes.'

'Keeping out of people's heads is just good manners.' She shot him a defiant look.

'I s'pose.' He shrugged, bruises biting. 'It's been a long day. For both of us. Let's go get some food. I'm starving.' Sighing, he stroked the floating mrug. Taking her hand, he pinged them away.

⋮

Scanning for the tmeg, then sending the mrug off to hunt, Ky was surprised to see Iago in the queue.

'Bananas, Iago. Where have you been?' Ky asked, grinning.

'Busy sorting things out. We've always looked after one another. Now we're all in need.' Iago waved a hand, smiling. 'This is good, eh? Centralising the catering is the simplest way for everyone right now. Only one set of people to hunt, to forage, to cook, leaving the others free for building. Only one patrol to be manned to keep away the predators. It works.'

'It's great. Can we push in?' Ky's stomach growled.

'That would be rude.' Fay shoved him from behind. His bruises shrieked. 'Besides, must wash up first.' Rolling her eyes, she tugged Ky away.

He scowled, stomach growling as it clenched.

'Pananas Fay. Lovely to see you.' Iago grinned at her, winking at Ky.

'But Iago, a tmeg-'

'See you later, Iago.' Fay tugged his arm.

'I want to ask you something!' Waving behind, Ky hurried off with her to the waterfall.

She found two clean bobonut shells from the stack.

'Peace offering.' She handed one to Ky. 'I know you hurt. Just ask, any time.'

Sharing a smile, they joined the queue by the fires. He noticed her scanning the sky again.

Iago had disappeared into the crowd. Shouts of greeting came from all directions, for both of them. Everyone already knew about his cabin. He wasn't so good at secrets as Fay.

The shuffling, smoky wait passed in sharing jokes and teasing about tmegs.

Pouting, he couldn't ask all the questions burning on his tongue.

Ky found it hard to concentrate over the clenching of his stomach. He wasn't used to building for so long in one day.

Eventually, a huge ladle of wine-dark vegetable stew was dropped in his bowl from one cauldron. Suddenly the big bobonut shell became so heavy he needed two hands to hold it.

At the griddles, a pile of cubes plopped into his stew. He couldn't see what any of it was, but the smell set his mouth watering.

At the end of the line, a round blue loaf was balanced on top. The fragrance of the fresh bread defeated him. He bent to take a bite, almost dropping his bowl.

'C'mon!' Fay scuttled toward a gap at the end of one table.

'Ky! Fay! Over here!' Fyl called.

Ky looked around to see the squadron sitting with him, shuffling to make space. His insides flipped. One day, he would be one of them.

Sliding onto the benches, quickly greeting the team, Ky tore off chunks, stuffing his mouth.

The conversation flowed around him as he hoovered up his dinner. He couldn't believe it. They treated him as if he belonged. Flavour filled his senses. Bubbles filled his head.

'Some of the cubes are chewy,' Fay mumbled, grimacing.

'Ha. When it tastes like that, who cares?' He smiled, mouth full, bubbles still popping.

Like the others around them, Ky had learned to save some of his bread to wipe the bowl at the end. For some reason, it made everyone laugh. Perhaps it was just the jostling elbows, or the fact that everyone seemed to do it together.

'It feels good to finish every dinner laughing.' He grinned at Fay. The team laughed, nodding.

'You will have to come for one of our

training sessions,' one of them offered.

'I'd like that.' Ky croaked, slack-jawed.

Winking, two team members departed with a wave. Ky looked down to hide his delight, sure he was floating off his seat.

'Look out!' Fay ducked. With darkness falling, pombats, roosting in the roof of the shelter, emerged, feasting on the night-time bugs it all attracted. Kittles, fire squirrels and flyers took care of the rest with the dawn. Iago was right. It worked.

'I needed that.' Grinning, rubbing his tight belly, he looked across at Fay.

'Me too.' She nodded, shooting nervous glances up at the pombats.

Ky grinned as someone belched loud. A chorus joined in from the remaining team and beyond.

'That was-' Fay grimaced.

'Cool.' A grubby face grinned further along the table. The child's big eyes flicked between them as he attempted to belch.

Ky reached across to high five, laughing.

The child stared, puzzled by his gesture.

'Oh.' Ky let his hand drop.

'Don't you be sicking up now Dav. Finish your food.' Fyl, his big brother, shoved him.

Fay smiled at the younger boy.

Scowling, Dav wisely returned to wiping his bowl.

'Good to see you, Fyl, and the team.'

'Ky's had a bad day.' Fay put in.

Glaring at her, Ky felt his cheeks burn.

'It's been rebuilt now.' He mumbled into his lap, loud enough to be heard. The eyes turned away. A tmeg attack obviously wasn't anything special for them.

'We have a barn if you need anything stored.' Fyl offered, hitching a brow.

'Oh, I-,' Ky stopped. He didn't use the chest much, just to keep special things in. He'd rather it was safe. 'I do have a chest I'd like to store, if you wouldn't mind.'

'No problem. Ping it here.' Fyl sent him an image of the barn door and the surroundings.

'Thanks. I will.' Ky nodded.

'We should–'

'I'm gonna find Zay.' With a dirty look at his brother, clutching his crust, Dav slid off the bench. He ran.

'Dav, get back here! Dav!' Rolling his eyes, Fyl took off after him, winding through the thinning throng.

'Fyl's a good guy.' Fay nibbled at her crust, eyes following his flying shadow as it disappeared into the darkness.

'Yup.' Ky nodded. The last of the team nodded too, laughing.

'The best,' said one, stretching. 'Well, I'm off.'

'Me too.' Saluting, they vanished. Ky's bubbles fizzed away.

'All this food has made me sleepy.' She stretched, yawning. 'Let's get a drink at the waterfall. Then I think I'm turning in.'

'Sounds good to me.' Ky suddenly realised everyone else had gone. The cooking fires had sunk to cinders, winking orange eyes. He hurried after her, into the dark.

The waterfall was a narrow stream trickling from the cliff. Another bobonut shell awaited the next person to hold it under the flow and drink their fill.

'Pa thinks we're almost at the level of Listeners.' Wiping her chin, Fay handed him the shell. Her voice drifted over the splash of the water, as if she were talking to herself.

'Listeners?' Hitching a brow, Ky found the cold shock easing his dry throat.

'They're sort of guardians, connected to the planet. There are lots of Legends about them. Kinda like MI5, listening to everything, dealing with threats, that sort of thing.' She flipped a hand, dipping the shell again.

'Threats? Ha. Everything's a threat here.'

'Not to us Mraxi. This is hard to explain. Things like alien crashes, like environmental problems, that kinda stuff.' Gulping it down, Fay shrugged, glancing up at the sky, offering him the shell.

'I thought the squadron did that?' Frowning, he took another gulp or two, handing it back. He couldn't see anything up there.

'They watch for it too. Listeners try to solve it or help us sort it out.' She filled the shell again.

'Awesome.' Grinning up at his mrug, the slopping sound jogged his memory. 'Did you find out about the fish?'

'Yes. They're eels.' Fay emptied the bowl, setting it back on its rock with a clatter. 'Night Ky.'

Then smirking, she was gone.

Grinding his teeth, he glared at the space where she'd been. She was still playing games.

A twig snapped in the trees behind him. Among the shadowed treetops, his eyes sought for spikes. Breathless, his heart slammed against his ribs. Time to go.

Shaking his head, he pinged back to his bed.

He may have rebuilt the cabin, but it was still just wood. The memory of it as a pile of splinters hung like a spectre at the back of his mind.

Something was bothering Fay too, another of her secrets, this time in the sky.

How could he ever sleep?

Yanking the blankets off his bed, he dragged them outside. The cave they'd sheltered in, down the valley would be the ideal place to hide his chest key. Maybe he'd even manage to sleep there too.

It would be back, he knew it.

16

⋮Mud⋮

Next morning, after a haunted night, the call came early.

'Mudslide casualties. All healers tonay.'

Fay scuttled off to help with the injured.

The team greeted her with stares.

'Don't say a word,' she snarled.

Glancing at each other, they rolled up their sleeves.

As each patient was healed and left, Fay,

soon floating with hunger, found her thoughts wandering.

She'd checked all her dream books, late into the nights, for mention of earthquakes, eclipses, black rain or mauve snow. She'd found none.

Fay sent off another grateful patient, washing her hands again.

A new person took their place. She lifted her hands and concentrated.

As tissue knitted, bones healed, she drifted again.

The eclipses, as something that happened more often with four moons, were in many dreams, always different, strange and ominous. Each time the creatures were driven to murderous frenzy.

Fay felt another surge of unease. Why should the coming eclipses be any worse than the previous ones? Why had Pa mentioned the Tower? Perhaps something was different.

She'd removed her hands before she

could surface, her patient turning to hug her, muddy face cracking into a smile.

'Thank you Fay. I love your hair. Please take my clip. If you ever come to the Dell, I'd love to see you...' She pressed something into her palm.

'You're welcome.' Fay smiled, watching her go.

Her empty stomach gurgled a protest. Another sound caught her ear.

Brushing off the shared mud, she popped her head out into the corridor, aware of a growing din.

Shoving the clip in her pocket, she set off toward the shouting. Grimacing, she spotted the fearsome Elder Ty, reach it first.

'I was only trying to help!' Myn jutted her chin, standing in a mess of tangled rope.

Fay scowled at her, stepping in with Fyl, reaching to unpick the knots.

'Don't come here again,' Ty, the shrunken Chief Healer snapped. 'And especially not with that!'

He stabbed a withered finger at the kittle, who jerked back against Myn's body, shaking.

'I can't imagine how you got it in, in the first place. And I don't believe you deserve to keep it.' The air around Ty crackled with fury.

Fay and Fyl shared a glance as more helpers joined them gathering up rope.

Backing away, Myn began to whine.

'I think you should go, Myn.' Fay shook her head.

The neglected baby mrug peed down her leg. Grimacing, she carried on unpicking with everyone else, as the warm puddle soaked in unnoticed.

'It was the kittle! He got excited and-,' Myn hopped on one foot, tears tracking down her cheeks.

'I'm sorry Myn. That pet is your responsibility. You have to learn to control it. Do some training.' Fay held up another knot.

'We were thrown out of that too!' wailed Myn.

'Do I need to walk you out?' Fay caught

up more dangling cords, narrowing her eyes.

The kitt made strangling noises in the silence, too tight again in Myn's grip.

'Still here? Well?' With a glare and a sniff, tiny Ty swept the offender out.

⋮

It was some time before Fay remembered the clip in her pocket. It felt smooth to her fingers as she pulled it into the light.

Shining silver, the smooth ear-shaped stone had somehow been melted into the shape of a long trumpet flower.

'It's beautiful!' Fay frowned. There was something familiar about it.

A flash of dread struck her like lightning.

17

┊Bones┊

'It came for me. I heard the twig snap. I'm sure of it.' Ky scooped tinga berries into his morning cereal at Central Eating, rubbing gritty eyes. No point mentioning his sleepless night in the cave. 'But why?'

'They don't hold grudges.' Fyl shrugged, frowning up at the stormy sky as he chomped. 'Perhaps you smell good.'

'At least you're not laughing, like Dad. There has to be something else.' Ky shook his aching head. 'Ah, here's Fay.'

Leaving Fyl with a wave, he headed back along the queue, ducking his head at a flash. Wind lashed his hair, splashing his face with a warning scatter of cold drops.

'It came for me last night.' Beside Fay, he sipped his juice to cover his whisper, wincing as the storm burned in his aching brain.

'The flitter?' Fay frowned, eyes distant, rubbing her temple. He caught her jump as lightning flashed and crackled again.

'The tmeg! Right here, remember?' Hissing, he rolled his eyes. The storm lashed the trees. A whirlwind of leaves crashed through the queue.

'Oh. Yes. Don't worry about it.' She winced as earsplitting thunder crashed overhead. 'We've had two flitters in a week in the clinic. That's unusual too. Must be all the upheaval. They're out of their usual habitat.' Shouting over nature's din, her hand shook as she scooped her cereal. He frowned. She looked different too. Better not mention it.

Another gust of wind whirled around them, twirling her hair like twin propellers, one long, one round. She staggered, shovelling food into her shell.

'But-,'

'All healers required, tonay.'

Ky winced at the clinic summons in his head. 'Oh no. But it's a Restday!'

'Mudslide. I've already healed some. See you later.' Shrugging, she pinged away, shell in hand.

Fyl waved, pinging away too.

Central Eating was suddenly a blur as half the people vanished.

Ky kicked a stump, licking his fingers clean. The mrug wheeled above in the boiling sky, riding the gale, keeping watch. Thunder boomed loud overhead. It swooped down to Ky's level. As thick needles of rain began to pelt down, he pinged them back to his cabin.

The grey day stretched ahead. It was a

111

welcome chance for a break, wasn't it? Perhaps he should try to sleep.

Staring out at the rain, he sucked his cheek. The tmeg would find him here, if he was right.

Below, the pale skeletons of the houses stood out, stark between the wet, jewel colours of the trees. That would be him, once the tmeg had finished with him. Bones.

Mum's face popped into his head. His lip twisted. He missed her hugs, hot chocolate and marshmallows. On Earth there were TV and games, no tmegs. But that would mean going to school, back to boredom and bullies. No thanks. He could be more use here.

Frowning, he rummaged in his back pack, pulling out some paper and a pen. If only he could talk to her. Dad seemed further away every day.

He settled on his bed, closing his eyes, waggling the pen in his fingers. Sighing, his neck drooped. He yawned. Fighting his body's weary sagging, he jerked upright. The tmeg must not catch him napping.

Someone could take her a letter next time they went. What should he say? Dad was never around when he needed him? There was nothing new about that. He had to find something positive to write.

The sound of the rain drumming on the roof drowned everything, even if the thunder had stopped. He wouldn't hear the tmeg coming.

Tugging his ear, he hopped back to the door to check. The air had turned to a steamy haze. He couldn't see very far. That dustbin smell would be washed away.

Rivers hurried along the path, lapping at the doorway to his cabin. He smiled to see slider slugs slipping down the hill, merry eye-stalks waving.

Maybe a tmeg wouldn't want to be out in this either.

The mrug didn't care, shooting outside. It swooped around the cabin, delighting in the teeming water, broadcasting joy. How could he do squadron training if he couldn't ride it?

Returning to his bed, he connected with it, using the mrug's eyes to check the surrounding forest. There was no sign of any large predator. Sighing, he took up the pen again, probing a sore spot on his chin.

'Hmmm. Dear Mum...'

That's when he heard it. A sound he'd only heard once before, in the dark, a distinctive, high pitched whine. Just tickling his ears, like a biter flying close in the dark. His heart began to thump. He felt sick.

Sitting up, he checked the floor, softly putting down his feet. Creeping to the doorway, he peered into the mist.

Way down the path, something was heaving beneath the sheen of the water. One long, crocodile-shaped head rose up from the stream.

'Eels too?!' Breathless, Ky grabbed his backpack, summoning the mrug.

He swung the pack onto his shoulder, looking round. Maybe it couldn't hear him.

The mrug wouldn't come, however many times he called.

The whining sound grew. The eels came closer, relentless.

Cold sweat trickled down his neck.

He called it again.

It swooped by, turning over in the air, mocking.

A lumpy head rose from the puddle by the stump.

Finally, he caught the mrug as it flipped by, pinging them both to the pond below Marnak; an open space where he could see them coming.

18

⋮Bump⋮

The boy limped into her room at the clinic, sighing relief as he sat again. Fay lifted his leg, setting a hand on his mud-crusted ankle.

'This won't take a minute.' She sank into his bones, rushed through his vessels. Something dark lurked there.

For a moment, she surfaced, wishing she could recall her words. Her empty stomach clenched.

'I'm Fay. What's your name?'

'Pery.' His smile was ghoulish. Death hung around him, inside him. She could taste it.

Pa had talked so calmly about death. For humans it was part of life, inevitable. On Mrax, especially for her, it was unthinkable.

Perhaps this was what her father meant.

She'd experienced the gaut's death. Life's fire inside fading to embers, then ashes. It haunted her. Her mouth dried up.

'Hold tight, then Pery.' She clenched her teeth, bracing herself for a fight.

⋮

She swam up a nightmare tunnel towards the light. It must be her feet flapping, kick, kick, kick...

She became aware of something knocking the back of her head, lifting feeble arms to fend it off.

Movement clicked her mind on. Whispering voices became clear. Frantic

117

hands were shaking her shoulders, bumping her head on the floor.

Slowly, Iyam's anxious face came into focus.

'Tmeg's teeth, girl. What have you done?'

'She healed my ankle.' Pery's smile flashed white above Iyam's shoulder.

Fay blinked around the forest of legs, mouth dry as ashes. The little mrug climbed onto her foot with a soft greeting.

'Sit her up. Here. Give her some room.' Many hands dragged her upright against the wall.

'Water...' she croaked.

The forest of trousers moved back. She blinked around the ring of concerned faces.

'Thanks.' Fay took the mug, gulping it down. She cleared her throat. 'How long was I-'

'I-I didn't know what to do. You were out for a while before I ran for help...Sorry.' Pery admitted.

'It's okay, Pery. Is your ankle alright now?'

118

she husked, frowning.

'Perfect.' He grinned, stamping.

'Well, I guess you can get off home, then. Take care.' Fay waved him away, despite Iyam's frown.

'Thank you Fay.' Eager, he pinged away.

'What's going on, Fay?' Iyam asked, teeth snapping.

'I saw death in him. I just couldn't let it...' Fay halted on a sob. She looked up at the ring of shocked, horrified faces. Tears leaked down her face.

'Ah! You're exhausted! Right, everyone out.' Iyam shooed everyone away, the beads in her hair rattling. 'You should have asked for help, Fay.'

'I didn't even think about it. Death has been haunting me lately. I had to get on with it...' Fay shook her head.

'Come on. Up you get.' Tutting, Iyam helped her to her feet once she'd wrapped the mrug back in position. 'Let's get you to your room and I'll fetch you some food. That should help.'

As Fay settled, boneless on her bed, Iyam left her to fetch the food.

She peeled off the mrug again, glad to be rid of the weight of it.

Once Fay had eaten the crust and slugcheese, draining the juice, Iyam set her hands on her forehead. Darkness sucked her down.

⋮

Awaking finally in the dark, Fay's brain felt on fire.

She'd dreamed of the moons, dancing in the sky, passing one another and looping back like flyers. Pa's warnings about the eclipses must be playing on her mind.

She sat up, yawning. Reaching up, she found her hair hadn't changed.

There was no way to tell if it was still daylight. Surely, she hadn't lost a whole day?

Her stomach grumbled. She clambered up, stretching, feeling restored.

In a sweet greeting, the mrug climbed over her foot. She wrapped it around her leg.

Smiling she sent a '*thankyou*' to Iyam.

After a visit to the washrooms, she sought out more food.

As she chomped the last corner of crust, Ky's voice rang in her head, asking where she was.

Smiling, she sent him a view of the entrance and went to meet him.

19

⁞Bounce⁞

The pond had doubled in size; the muddy water came up to his knees. It was still raining; fat drops exploding up on impact. Ky shivered, instantly soaked. After the cold prickle of a ping, that was all he needed.

'Hey!'

The mrug plunged in, splashing him with one grumpy corner, flipping away.

The amber willow where his dad used to

fish, made a little island now, rather than leaning on the edge.

He took shelter underneath it, perching on the lumpy roots, watching for eels, casting out to hear what the mrug was thinking. Excitement was all that came through.

From here, he had a good view to Marnak on the hill above.

The grand colonnade of stone beasts had toppled. Huge, oblong chunks of rock lay everywhere like forgotten dominos. Walls bulged or sagged with corners shaken down.

He had seen the devastation in his mind the day they pushed the planet out of its destructive orbit. Everyone involved could see it then; storms, earthquakes, fire. It was quite different being here now, part of it.

He shivered, rubbing a shaking hand over his face. That's why he was here. To help.

He jumped as a bolt of lightning streaked down the sky.

'Sitting under a tree in a storm. Not a great idea.'

He sent out a call, slapping the surface of the water.

After a moment, the mrug returned, chewing, broadcasting happiness.

He reached down, flinching as lightning flashed again. It dodged away. How was he ever going to join the squadron if he couldn't control his mrug?

A mis-matched pair of eyes popped up where it had been.

'What the -?' Ky stared. He leaned forward for a closer look, slipped. 'Ah!' He plunged in head first.

Blinded by mud, he surfaced choking. Struggling to his knees, he wiped his eyes clear. He checked all around for the ominous spikes of a tmeg, sighing when he found none.

Picking out weed tangled in his hair, he snagged the mrug. Maybe it was cold, but that felt like a giggle.

Grim, he waded away from the tree, out of the water.

Released, the mrug floated above him like an umbrella. His mud-streaked clothes clung to his skin. The new sandals Fay had found him at the clothes bank were probably ruined.

Forging up the slippery hill, his teeth began to chatter. He could barely see through the rain. At least it was washing off the mud when the mrug flew too far ahead.

'Fay? Are you still working?' Ky picked his way between the rocks.

There was no reply. The window in her mind was frosted.

Climbing over debris now, he was almost to shelter. He hopped down off a huge chunk of caramel stone, clambered through the broken stumps of the colonnade, the slumped walls. Tugging an ear, he made for the Great Hall.

One corner had crumbled. The roof had caved in on that front corner. People crowded at the other end.

At the back, they were singing, sheltered from the storm. Huddled together, arms around shoulders and smiling, some were even trying to dance, or at least jiggle to the rhythm.

He didn't recognise anyone but the music was like a magnet. He tapped his phone to record.

Beckoning, a woman put out an arm, pulled him in. It was like a giant hug.

Everyone steamed, sharing body heat and some less pleasant smells. Warm again, Ky didn't care.

The unfamiliar song wove through his head, made him bounce too.

The mrug circled above them, seeming to flap in time with the tune.

The woman caught his arm again.

'Are you-' She stopped.

The song cut off.

Everyone winced at one final clap of thunder that shook the walls. Through the gap in the ceiling, Ky caught one last, dim flash.

The rain stopped. In the sudden hush, Ky

caught that sound again, above the trickle and drip, the high-pitched whine. He stopped recording, jamming his phone away. They were coming.

'*Fay? Where are you?*'

'*I just finished. You can meet me here, if you like.*' She sent a picture of the entrance to the clinic.

'Gotta go. Thanks for the er, music.' Ky peeled himself away from under the woman's arm.

Water seemed to be rising up in the doorway. Hairs stood to attention all over his body. One day, he'd notice too late to escape.

Everyone had laughed when he mentioned the tmeg. Perhaps he was imagining it. Perhaps not.

Ky summoned his mrug. For once, it came down immediately. Touching it, he pinged them away, convinced that nowhere was safe.

20

⋮Fun⋮

'I thought we could have a little fun.' Fay suggested when he arrived, bouncing.

'What sort of fun?' Ky scratched his head, dubious as always. 'You look er, different.'

He looked up at the mrug circling above, as if it would know why.

'How about some shale skiing?' Ignoring his comment, Fay grinned, grabbing a couple of woollen wraps from the rack by the door.

'What-?' He gawped.

'Come on!' She pinged them all away, giggling.

⋮

The wind was strong at the top of the mountain, fleeting fragrances snatched from her nose. In the sunshine, Panchak's snowy peak loomed glistening nearby. Eagles called up here, above the churning storm clouds. The valley far below was lost in dark mist.

'Put this on.' Shivering, she handed him one wrap, shrugging into the other. 'This way.'

Following the path worn by generations, they emerged round the peak to a deceptively smooth slope that vanished into the cloud layer below. Far away, the tapering top of the Tower pierced through. She smiled.

'This mountain's like a cheese wedge.' Ky commented, staring around as his mrug turned lazy circles in the sky.

'Sort of, I suppose. Now, check down

here. It looks straight down, doesn't it? But if you look carefully there are little level bits, ledges to the sides, where you can stop if you need to. Where the tufty grass is. See?' She pointed.

After a moment, he nodded.

'Will I need them?' he asked, tugging his ear.

'Well, I won't. But you get up quite a speed. So if it's too much, or you feel out of control, you can slow it down by stopping.'

'Oh. I see. So what do we sit on?'

'Sit! Ha. Only babies sit. We stand up. That's why it's called skiing.' Fay laughed, heaving out a couple of slices of stone from the stack behind a gnarled bush. 'See?' They were worn shiny.

'Just one square to stand on?' He eyed the thin slab, running his fingers along the ragged edge.

'Yup.' She bent to tug out some sticks from the pile.

'More like snowboarding then.' Ky

nodded. 'I'm used to a skateboard. How different can it be?' He grinned, finally.

'Here.' She shoved two twisted sticks in his hand, settling the mrug on her leg. With familiar skill, she set her fingers into the worn grips of her own. Ky stared.

'You don't have sticks for snowboarding.' He offered them back.

She wasn't letting go of hers now.

'Your choice.' Shrugging, Fay set her square at the edge of the field of loose pebbles. Eager, she stepped on. 'But they're good for fending off any unwanted attention.' She nodded at a curious slinker emerging on the rocks above.

'Oh.' Ky set his slate down, stepping on. 'Whoa!' He slid on the shifting surface, windmilling his arms. Fay giggled as he jumped off, the slab slipping away down the slope. The slinker vanished.

'Take another.' She waited while he pulled one out and set it down again.

He took a great huff of scented mountain

air and smiled. 'This is more like a Restday should be.'

'Let's go!' Grinning, Fay pushed off, letting the loose shale take her. Wind tugged her hair, numbed her nose and slapped her cheeks.

'Wahoo!' Ky was riding beside her, sticks tucked under one armpit, the other arm raised for balance.

Grit sprayed as he carved his way zigzag down the slope, yelling.

Fay followed in a sedate straight line, laughing as he bent, then stretched back, flailing.

'You're great at this!' she yelled, angling her feet for greater speed. She didn't care who won, did she?

'It's amazing!' He hooted, beaming.

'All that zig-zagging's slowing you down.' She called as she caught up. 'See?'

'Watch this then!' He shot away, vanishing between swirling wraiths of mist.

Fay plunged in too. Moisture beaded on

her skin, chilling it further. Ghosts seemed to crowd in around her. Drops gathered on her lashes, flying off as they grew.

'Fay? You alright?' His voice was muffled by the fog. Either that or he was way ahead now.

'I'm fine. We should be out of it in a minute. It's thicker than I remember.'

'This is longer than a minute, isn't it? No creatures will come into this will they?' His voice floated back.

'I reckon wildlife has more sense.'

Now they were skiing blind, trusting to gravity.

'Wow what a view! Yahoo!' Ky's shout brought a wave of relief. The mist thinned around her, melted to wisps trailing in her wake. Then it was gone.

Sunset filled the sky with blinding gold. Far below them the river was a tangled copper thread in the valley.

Down she slid, after Ky's shrinking shape. It was harder to see in this light, easy to miss the ledges and tufts that might trip you. She shifted closer to the centre, squinting.

Below, the sloping forest glades were lit by the brassy glare. Above, flocks of flyers wheeled, wind-blown, peppering the vastness of sky.

The wind was no longer as icy down here, drying her damp face and hair. The mrug clung on, a lead weight she had to balance by leaning.

'Watch out!' Ky's yell from below made her slow, tipping her slab back.

Sliding up a rise, she felt the problem through her feet. The ground shook beneath her. An earthquake!

Turning her head she glanced back up the slope. The shale was dancing behind her, a wave of it rushing down towards her.

'Avalanche!' she yelled, speeding up, digging in the sticks.

'This way.' Ky swung an arm as he swooped left.

Fay angled her feet, peeking back again.

The wave was growing.

She rocked, urging herself faster, leaning against the weight of the mrug.

Ky had carved a path through for her to follow.

She fought for balance, pushing hard with her sticks.

The wave was almost upon her, rearing up. A sound like thunder grew behind her.

She swung toward Ky, waiting in the shadows beneath a ledge, beckoning.

The thunder roared, licking at her heels.

Ky snatched her in.

The wave rumbled over them, spewing out in a waterfall of stone. Dust billowed.

'Thanks.' She clung to him, panting.

They began to chuckle.

'That was amazing.' He laughed. 'Do we have time to go again?'

21

⫶Scale⫶

'Ky! There you are. Why aren't you in the cabin?'

'Uh?' Yawning, Ky scratched through his tangled curls, trying to fight off the itching from his interrupted rolling log nightmare. 'Feels like I only just went to sleep. How'd you find me?'

'Mrugs talk, you know. Ky, something's happened at Pa's barn.' Fyl couldn't stand still.

'You need me?' Ky yawned.

'Pa says the barn's wrecked!' Fyl tried to tug the blanket off him. 'Your chest is there, remember?'

Silhouetted against the dawn, Ky spotted his mrug hovering behind Fyl in the doorway.

'Wrecked?' He rubbed his eyes, frowning.

'Come on!' Fyl shoved his clothes at him, tapping his foot.

'What about-,' Ky's suddenly dry tongue stuck to the roof of his mouth.

Dragging the tunic over his head, it caught, jamming his neck. 'Argh!'

Fyl yanked it down with an impatient hand.

Ky's stomach gurgled a symphony as he jumped into trousers.

'Eat later.' Fyl set a hand on his shoulder, snatching him and his mrug away.

⋮

Only the tall stone ends stood, crumbling

around the edges, in a sea of splinters. Ky stared at the familiar sight, shaking with sudden cold.

Fyl's family had already started clearing the mess away.

'Pananas, Fyl and friend. Welcome.' Pa Gwyn shook his head. 'I've never seen this, all my life.'

'This is Ky, Pa. He's joining the squadron soon. What did this?' Fyl gawped at the wreckage.

'No time to worry about that. Another storm's coming this way. C'mon.' Gwyn trotted away, Fyl close behind.

Feeling sick, Ky followed, itching to help. His cabin had looked the same.

Fyl and his Pa, his sister Nymba and mother Naya, Dav and his friend Zay were all inside, picking up splinters.

'We'll be falling over one another in here. Get out, Nit!' Gwyn lifted their gangly kittle towards Ky. It landed on its toes, prancing away with a sniff.

'See if you can find any tracks, Ky.' Fyl called.

The flyers were singing. He tiptoed around the area, watching the trees.

The mrug caught a flyer in the next field, settling to a meal.

Ky's jealous stomach gurgled. Fat berries dangled on a bush, amber and inviting. He didn't know what they were. Better not.

He came to the lake where the mrugs had their babies. A thousand red eyes watched him. In the mud at the edge was the print of just one giant tmeg toe, a gouge at the tip from the claw. Ky shuddered.

Catching up, his mrug dived in, touching wings, rolling somersaults in the water.

Joy blossomed in Ky's head. Smiling he left it there.

Finally, he found a clue, a little way off. A scale embedded in the damaged bark of a tree, leaning out the ground.

Clawed roots still clung in the damp soil.

His fingers grazed the bark as he reached up for the scale. Pain seared through his brain. He snatched his hand away.

Frowning, he focused on the tree, drew it upright, set the roots back into the ground. He stamped the soil back down.

After a moment, he raised a wary hand. His fingers touched the rough bark. Pleasure glowed through him, warm and fragrant.

The bark seemed to squirm. The scale dropped into his arms.

He stared down at it, catching the brooding colours of the storm sunrise in its pearly surface. He remembered that glow on the tmeg's scales with a shudder. There were so many scaled creatures here.

Pulling his ear, he hefted it under his arm, heading down to help the family.

He stopped at the lake for the mrug. It seemed happy to see him, soaring out into the air, circling him, dripping.

Over by the barn, Fyl beckoned. Setting the scale down under a shrub, Ky rolled up his sleeves.

Between them, they saved some of the hay and grain, floating it to cover beneath the trees as the clouds darkened.

Ky worked with them, hunting out the scattered tools and containers.

Nymba sang as they worked, joined by Naya, lifting their gloom. Ky didn't know the song. Dav and Zay piped up too. Fyl yelled out the chorus, laughing. Nit came back to bounce around them.

Grim, Gwyn sparked a bonfire of the splintered wood.

Eventually, Ky found his heavy metal chest a distance away under a bush. It had cracked right across. There were fresh gouges on its surface. He sighed to see the lock had held it together, then gulped. He had brought this on them.

'I have to tell you-,' Dragging it into the farmhouse, he bumped into Gwyn.

'You know something?'

'This is my fault. It was after my chest.'

Ky scuffed a foot in the dirt.

'Ha! There's no accounting for the beasts, boy. They have no need for chests! You can't blame yourself.'

'Look at it. It tried to open it.' Ky pointed.

'Maybe it was curious.' Gwyn shrugged.

'I found something!' Fyl's voice rang out from the paddock.

They all charged towards him. He pointed at a brown pile by his feet.

'It came back again.' Scowling, Ky bent to examine the dung, stabbed a long splinter into it.

'Again?' Fyl straightened from his search. 'How many times?'

'It smashed up the cabin once before.' Ky shrugged. 'I found this scale over there in a tree.' He tugged the scale out from beneath the shrub.

Gwyn snatched it, glancing up as rain began to patter.

'That's tmeg alright.' He turned it in his hands, staring from it to Ky.

142

'I'll take my chest home, just in case.' Ky gnawed his lip.

'What have you done?' Hand on his hair, Fyl's eyebrows shot up.

'Nothing! I don't know. I don't even know if it's always the same tmeg.'

'It's more than unlucky.' Fyl shook his head.

'Can't be a coincidence.' Gwyn stared at the scale as lightning flashed too close and thunder cracked the sky.

Ky's empty stomach quaked.

22

¦Spooked¦

Fay sighed, drooping from her work day. Perhaps Mrax was finally getting to him. It must be hard, when all he'd known was Earth.

'I can feel them coming.' Ky's voice trembled through the steaming trees.

'I can understand-,' she began, only to be cut off with another rant about Fyl's barn. Rolling her eyes, she scanned the cloudy sky.

She pressed her lips together, stomping

into the soft ground.

He'd never been like this before. Even his mrug had left him.

'You can't possibly! It's different for me.' He was tugging both ears now. Flyers were beginning to pick up the tone and copy it, not that he'd notice. She bit down a smile.

Fay took a deep breath. 'Maybe you need to go see your mum.'

'I'd just freak her out. Besides, she's coming soon, Dad says.' Suddenly, his eyes shone.

'She is?' Fay felt her jaw drop. She hadn't expected that to happen, ever.

A flyerbug whizzed past. Reflexively, she snapped her mouth shut.

'Dad's built her a whole new home. I think she'll love it.' His tone had changed, for the better.

A shaft of sun shot through the leaves. She smiled.

'Let's go eat and you can tell me all about it.'

⋮

Fay watched Ky mop his stew, combing her fingers through her straight hair. Grinning at last, a tiny Elder took their seat, centre stage. She gawped in surprise.

'I thought we missed this last night,' she hissed, nudging Ky.

The children scuttled forward to sit around his feet.

'This is what you need,' she hissed, feeding a morsel to her mrug. 'Without the privilege of hearing all our Legends from early childhood, you're missing all this. It's life-saving knowledge.'

Ky scowled.

'Apologies for not coming last night, I was, er, detained. So as a special treat, tonight we explore the Legend of the Gauts and the Geeble.'

The voice came through, soft and lilting in her head. Smiling, everyone settled to silence.

'Many of you will have grown up with the

old stories of the gauts. You will know the Greatness of Glim, the Trials of Gavinn, the Tales of Gnashers and Gauts.'

A flitter trumpeted in the distance, breaking through the expectant hush. Someone burped loud and the children broke into tittering. Fay spotted some healers sitting with the squadron nearby. Ky probably hadn't noticed them yet. The Elder had to wait to continue.

'As you know, the gauts live in the seas. They are gentle creatures and occasionally our heroes. But this story is one you may not know. For the geeble is a ferocious creature, always hungry and an unlikely ally for the gauts. But the gauts had a problem. A hopping sea squirt had evolved and multiplied.' His wispy eyebrows rose at the doubtful muttering. 'What's this? You don't think a squirt could live in the sea?'

'Maybe the question should be; why had it evolved to live there? We later discovered that there was a new fungus, perhaps of alien origin, which was killing all the squirts on land.'

'Aww.' The children all groaned.

'So every sensible squirt fled to the sea to survive. Each spawning in the waves meant the next generation adapted to the new environment, and soon the new species thrived there.'

Children whooped and clapped, jumping around.

'They devoured land bugs and sea bugs, keeping the numbers down. But their amphibian slime coated the rocks and children began to slip on it. So there you find our tale, mysterious and sad.'

Clicks of encouragement brought a smile to the Elder's face.

'But you don't want to know, really, do you?' The Elder made to turn away, his small, craggy frame lit by the cook fires. He flicked a dark look back at the deepening shadows.

The children all hooted, yelling for him to come back. Smiling, he resumed his seat.

'Oh you do! Well. The gauts are a proud and noble race. We are pleased to call them our siblings of the sea. But the squirts were attacking them, nibbling their tendrils. Now, you may not know that their capes are precious to the gauts. Apart from keeping them warm they are an indicator of good health and status. The highest in their society have the broadest capes. They believe their capes have special powers. So as you can imagine, anything nibbling their tendrils may well work up to the capes, and that would be most unwelcome!'

Fay thought back to the gaut on the beach, blinking away tears.

The children snapped their teeth, pretending to nibble.

'So the nibbling squirts became a problem. They seemed to love the taste of the tendrils and the gauts worried. They meant the squirts no harm. All they wanted was for them to leave them alone. The situation went on and worsened, with no

149

communication between the gauts and the squirts.'

The adults shook their heads. The children clicked encouragement. Smiling, Fay fed her mrug a crumb of bread.

'Then one day, their precious Princess Gwenna lost a huge chunk of her wondrous tendrils to a squirt. The tiniest corner of her cape broke free from her shoulder. The Princess fell unconscious. It was the catalyst that changed everything.'

Hiding her wet face, Fay wiped her nose on her sleeve. The children fell still and silent. Anticipation hung in the air.

'A brave young gaut called Giligon came up with an ingenious plan. He had a talent for communicating with the smallest creatures of the sea. He gathered thousands of them together, close to the squirts' hunting grounds. Once the squirts began to feast, he led the bugs out into deep water, knowing the hungry squirts would follow. He laid down his life for the Princess.'

'Aaah.' Everyone called, together.

'Yes. He led them far, far out. A long train of all the greedy squirts came swimming behind. And there, in the deeps, he found what he sought. A geeble.'

Dav grabbed Zay close to make two heads, honking. The children giggled. The Elder flapped his hands to settle them down. Sniffing, Fay felt a smile twitch at her lips.

'Poor Giligon could not reach the geeble as it rushed to the surface. Its mind full of hunger and anger, it rose up, jaws agape to harvest this feast. The two heads snapped and gulped down everything that lived. Brave Giligon was lost.'

The children groaned in chorus. The wizened Elder smiled.

'The Gauts were saved, for the squirts were gone. The Princess awoke soon after, her cape healed. They declared Giligon a hero and still teach their new generations to follow his example of selfless sacrifice.'

The audience clapped their knees in

appreciation. Clumsy, Fay smacked her mrug on the nose as she moved her hands. It took its revenge, hot down her leg. Ew.

Dav and Zay danced, giggling, sandwiched tight together.

'So this is the legend of The Gauts and the Geeble.' He bowed deep for the applause. 'Before I go, I should advise everyone to spread the warning that we are expecting eclipses to begin soon. They will trigger more extreme earthquakes and send all the creatures into panic. The worst creatures from the deep will emerge, slithers will swarm. We recommend you stop work, staying safe inside until the light resumes and the noise returns to normal. A good evening to you all.'

With a glower at Dav, the Elder departed.

'Another Legend for you.' Fay flapped her wet trouser leg, swiping her face with her tunic sleeve.

'Eclipses.' Ky whispered, lost in thought.

Fay looked around for a familiar face. Fyl

was just collaring Dav, no doubt to take him home. Most people were vanishing, blurring in the gloom.

Soon they were the last.

'C'mon Ky. Everyone's gone.'

He was still lost to her, staring off towards the moon, half asleep or maybe listening. He would probably sit there all night.

He didn't have a cold, wet leg. She nudged him in the ribs.

'Ky! You need sleep. Time to go.'

He blinked at her, ghostly pale. His eyes were panda-dark pits.

Had he heard a word of the Legend or the warning?

Something roared close by.

'Are slithers eels?' He whispered.

'No they're like big snakes, mostly from deep caves.'

'Oh. Marvellous. Night.' He muttered, vanishing.

A tree shivered behind her.

B. Random

Fay pinged home, chewing her lip. She'd never seen him so spooked.

23

┋Flip┋

Next morning after another almost sleepless night in the cave, Ky woke from his nightmare with a headache. Stashing his bedding back in the cabin, he pinged to Central Eating to gorge. He saw no familiar faces as he filled his shell, not even healers. The squadron must still be out on patrol. He'd have to get used to a different regime once he joined them.

Returning from his feast, the mrug settled to the ground outside the cabin, rolling its eyes.

'What is it?' Yawning, Ky stared down at it, frowning at the rush of excitement from it echoing in his head. He drooped, wishing he'd been able to sleep.

The mrug flipped a corner, sending him a sudden rushing feeling, like flying through the air. Transparent lids flashed over its scarlet eyes.

'You want me to get on?' He gasped, feeling a flutter in his chest. 'I don't want to hurt you. Are you sure?'

Biting his lip, he stepped closer, feeling the ache pound between his temples.

'You know this is what I've been dreaming of, don't you? The squadron are waiting for us...' His heart thumped. His mouth dried up.

It flipped that corner again, the long tendrils trailing over the edges.

'Are you big enough to hold my weight now?' Tugging an ear, he fought back screaming images of crashing to the ground, cabin walls, water.

The huge, excited red eyes gazed up at him. Gingerly he knelt beside it, sliding one hand over its ridges, lifting his knee onto its leathery back.

With contact, another surge of sensations swamped him. Crushing. Bruising.

'Ow.' With a flip, the mrug dumped him in a bush, shooting away.

'Hey! It was your idea!' Ky roared after it.

The bush leaned, crunching. He began to slither. Head snapping round, he felt the edge of the cliff slide under his body. Grabbing wildly at branches, his feet swung out into space.

'Ah!' Twigs and leaves showered his face as he struggled for a grip. Staring down at the void between his feet, he scrabbled, panting.

Gulping he heaved, feeling his arms and shoulders burn. The bush ripped and shredded. He inched up, gasping.

After an age, his flailing feet found a

ledge. He kicked himself to safety, flopping on the grass, panting. It felt like an army of wasps drilled into his head.

The hovering mrug soared up into the sky, oozing distress.

Rubbing his dusty elbow, Ky stomped back to the cabin, chin wobbling.

His dreams would never come true.

He should have stayed in bed.

24

⋮Fried⋮

The call came before breakfast, waking her from tortured dreams. Three men and a kittle arrived in the clinic early. The silent men were clutching various burn injuries. The kittle was yowling at the top of its lungs.

The healers took a person each, which left Fay, yawning, with the kittle.

Its fur was matted and filthy. Thinking it

was wild, she snagged its legs in both hands before it could run, looping a cord around them. Digging her fingers through the dense, matted coat, she couldn't feel any breaks in the delicate bones. Kittles were all fur.

She stared into the fried egg eye. Something in its expression felt familiar.

'Fry? Is that you?' The broad tongue lolled. It licked her hand.

'Let's get you cleaned up then.' She carried it to the bathing room. It began to fight her grip, head whipping.

'Oh, no you don't! Myn said you didn't like baths. But you never had a bath like mine, Fry. You'll love this.'

Pulling out the bung, she let the water stream in.

Fry watched it, trembling with terror. Its eye stretched even bigger.

She stroked it, cooing. Slowly it began to relax, flopping over her arm, bright, jade eyelids drooping over its eyes.

She took up the tongs, dropping a hot

stone from the fire-grate into the water. It rattled, dancing. The water began to steam gently.

Terrified, Fry thrashed those legs, releasing the cord, knocking over the blimworm stand, almost plunging them into darkness.

As Fay tried to set it right, Fry twisted again in her grip, sliding out of her grasp. It bounced her over, leaping straight onto the fire grate.

As she rose to her knees, its yowls hurt her ears, echoing off the cave walls.

Every hair on her body rose as the ghost of a dream trampled over her. Shaking in the gloom she gasped as the embers caught in its fur.

'Fry. Stop!' She lunged for it with a blanket. The creature was in serious pain now. Its screams were pitiful as it cannoned off the walls, danced frantic on the ceiling.

That sound brought her cold sweat to bead and trickle.

She tripped over the blanket, crashing into the wall. 'Ow!'

Shoving the blimworm stand upright, chin jutting, she grabbed a wet cloth.

As it thwacked off the nearby wall, she snagged it in mid-air, folding it close to pat out the flames on its head. Instantly she plunged it, still wrapped, into the bath.

Fry went rigid, quivering, not breathing. She held it there to make sure the fires were out, talking to it softly.

Probing its mind, its thoughts were like fireworks.

Cautiously, she added some soothing herb-oil. The lemony scent filled the room, yet still the kittle lay stiff as a surfboard in her arms.

Slowly, she tried to peel away the cloth. Blackened fur came with it, floating on the surface like a raft. Fry gazed at her, stunned, shaking. She bit her lip, pausing.

'It's okay Fry. At least the dirt and matting burned off...' She lifted it out, onto the bench, patting it gently dry with another cloth.

Finally, she peeled it away. Slowly, the damage was revealed. Very little fur remained. Fry had a few lilac tufts left, one on its head, one at the end of its tail.

In between it reminded her of an earth stick insect, singed and blistering. Even the curved, wide nails that it walked on were black. There was nowhere she could lay her hands that wouldn't hurt.

'Oh Fry...' Fay winced, biting her lip.

The kittle tipped its head to look down at itself. Its mouth gaped. Drool spun down in long threads.

She watched a gulp chase down the long, thin neck, reaching out to heal.

Fry let out a long, tortured howl.

'I hear you Fry!' Myn fell in the doorway, panting.

Fay felt the warmth drain from her face. Quickly she plastered on a stiff smile.

'Oh. Fay!' Her round face lit up. 'You have it. I'm-,'

She took in the rigid pet drooling on the bench. She turned ghostly pale.

'Fay? That is Fry, right?'

'Yes, I'm afraid the crazy kitt leapt into the fire. It'll take a while for its fur to grow back. Perhaps you can hold it while I put some cream on those burns.'

'Oh.' Myn grabbed her pet, none too gently. Fry squawked.

'Careful. Burns hurt.' Fay chided, picking up the pot of bobonut cream.

She began to daub it onto the charred skin feeling the poor kitt flinch each time. Blisters were erupting, growing like feeding ticks between the patches of raw, weeping skin.

Finally, she touched one spot too many. Fry, now covered in cream and drool, slid out of Myn's grip and was gone, yowling.

'Fry!' Yelled Myn, chasing after it.

Sighing, Fay sat back as the door flap slapped closed behind them.

Chilling memories drifted there, in the

back of her mind.

Fry had suffered in a similar way to those kittles in the dream but there was no fire there.

Rubbing her arms, she wondered how long it would be, before that dream stopped haunting her.

25

⁝Bloodshot⁝

'On the way with Mum. Meet us at the house.'
Dad's voice rang in his sore, sleepless head.

Dropping his log on the pile, Ky pinged to the treehouse.

He was early. Twitching in a chair, he tapped a foot.

'Fay, Mum's coming now. I'm gonna miss breakfast.' He didn't care.

The view from Dad's deck across the

valley toward that glimpse of sunset sea made him smile.

Sitting there, doubts crowded in. What if some new disaster were about to take place?

Sighing, he kicked his heels, rubbing his temples. His mind was a pounding tornado of what-should-he-dos, about the tmeg, Dad, Mum, Earth.

His parents materialised on the deck.

'Ky!' His mother, still staggering from the journey, held out her arms.

'I have so much to tell you...' He clutched her fragile bones, sharing a concerned glance with his dad. She still looked thin.

'Oh, I've missed you so much!' She smothered his face with kisses

'Me too.' He backed away a little, smiling, feeling better.

'Let me look at you.' Balzar supporting her, she stood back, inspecting him. 'You've grown up. You're not my little boy any more.' She burst into tears.

'Hey, hey.' Balzar led her inside. 'No need

for that.'

'It's alright Mum. You're here now.' Ky sat beside her, patting her trembling hands, chewing his tortured lips. His headache surged, worse than ever. Dad was here. Why did he still feel like her tears were his fault?

Balzar went to make her tea.

'Mum, I have so much to show you.' Ky tried again, as Mum snorted loud into a tissue.

'Sorry. It's all a bit...' Her bloodshot eyes looked past him at the windows. 'Oh, my.'

'Dad's made you this wonderful tree house.'

'It's...magnificent!' She tipped her head to take in the trees at the corners with their dangling leaves and the soaring rafters above. Somehow Balzar had turned the roots upward to form the walls. Could he do that?

'I made it especially for you.' Handing her a mug of steaming tea, Balzar settled beside her. He squeezed an arm around her narrow shoulders. 'OK now?'

'Feel so silly.' Sipping she nodded, resting her cheek on his arm. 'I never jumped space before. It shakes you up.' She laughed.

'My mrug used to hate it.' Ky nodded, remembering its reaction the first few times, shaking and leaking everywhere. 'It gets easier, don't worry.'

'Ha. Just what we always said to you, I know. It doesn't work, does it?' Her laugh had a catch in it.

Ky met his dad's frowning eyes.

A leaf floated from one of the dangling branches, scraping the silence as it hit the floor. She jumped.

'It's just a leaf. Nothing to worry about.' Balzar took her empty cup. 'I made this place to be a fortress. Nothing can get through the wood or the glass. You're safe in here. Come, I'll show you.' He held out a hand to help her up.

Ky hesitated, pouting.

'C'mon.' Mum held out a hand. 'It's been so long since we spent time together, I want you beside me.'

With a little glow, Ky rose, curling her fingers between his. His headache vanished.

⁝

It felt, for a while, as if they were a proper family again. He smiled as they laughed together. It felt like old times, ancient history. His Earth life seemed a distant memory.

Even so, leaving was torture; abandoning her smiles and those hugs he'd been missing.

She wanted him to stay.

Dad wanted him to go, he could tell.

⁝

Back at the cabin, he stood staring across the valley. No ominous spikes showed through the tree tops. He tugged an ear, feeling the headache return.

Was this how it was going to be now? Would he always feel an outsider?

26

⋮Target⋮

Next morning, Central Eating was almost deserted. Fay spotted Ky pinging in just after her, heading straight for the cereal tubs.

'Pananas Ky! I missed you.' Frowning, she caught him up.

'Bananas, Fay. You're late today.' His usual grin was absent. 'I'm starving.'

Grabbing a shell, he filled it fast, scooping tinga berries into his mouth at the same time.

'Me too.' Fay waited her turn, tapping her foot. She stared at the panda shadows around his eyes.

'Oh, Mum's here.' Moving along, Ky dropped a generous splat of yoghurt on his cereal. Gobs of it flew down his tunic. He didn't seem to notice, so intent on stuffing it in his mouth

'You seem distracted. Something wrong?' Fay scooped cereal, watching his pale face.

'Bad start,' he mumbled through his mouthful, glancing up at the mrug. 'A few bad starts.'

'Me too. Problems with Fry, Myn's kittle.' She led the way to a seat.

'First there was trouble at Fyl's barn.' Ky gulped loud. 'A tmeg smashed it up.'

The words seemed to freeze him. He stared at his shell, pushing it away.

'You know it was a tmeg? It's hard to believe it could happen again.' She squeezed berries between her teeth, letting the sweet juice ooze through.

'Yup.' Ky bent, hefting something from under the table. 'Found it wedged in tree bark nearby.' He clunked it down on the table.

Fay leaned forward. The huge, fluted scale glinted gold around the edge. She nodded. ''S tmeg alright.'

His haunted eyes locked with hers, as if she could tell him what to do. They settled on her hair.

She gritted her teeth.

'I think you need to take your mind off it.' She shrugged.

'How?' Ky slumped, holding his head in his hands. 'I can't sleep. Even at work I'm scanning all day.'

'You could make your Mum a gift.' Fay pondered.

'I saw her yesterday. Must be too early for breakfast yet.' Ky's smile faded. 'Dad gets her everything...'

Fay's eye caught his mrug floating above the clearing.

'Have you ridden that mrug yet? Fyl said

you could start now, didn't he?'

'He did…' Scowling, Ky gazed up at his circling friend, a dark, diamond shape in the sky.

'What are you waiting for? You could be cruising the skies!' She grinned down at the pale mrug on her leg, wishing it would grow faster.

'But what about the tmeg?' Ky wailed.

She rolled her eyes.

'All healers report to clinic tonay. Injured narth.' The call clanged through her head. An image of acres of angry, speckled pink flesh filled her head.

She stood, masking a flicker of relief.

'I have to go back to work. Do something new! See you later.'

She pinged, despite his thunderous expression.

After all these centuries, no tmeg would target one person, would it?

27

⋮Fly⋮

Ky pinged back to the cave to stash the scale, then on to the broken valley to start his workday scavenging. Storms overnight had left it soggy and dripping. Huffing sweet, fresh-washed air, he stumbled over the rubble to a stone cottage that had crumbled at one corner. It was too small to fit a tmeg.

Creaking in the breeze, the door flap hung

open. The roof was askew, but looked intact. He squinted at it. Perhaps he could lift the whole thing to the next valley.

First, as usual, he had to be sure no creature had moved in. Everything shone or sparkled, blinding under the clear sky as he listened. The only shadow came from his mrug, cruising overhead.

Ky set a cautious foot in the doorway. Blinking, he waited until he could see. Was that just the breeze moaning through gaps in the stones? No, it was some weird flyer singing. That was a good sign.

Breathless, he took another slow step into the dimness. A tmeg was too big to hide in here. Nothing scuttled or hissed.

Scratching his head, he inspected the piles of twigs, splintered wood, tangled fabric and stones. Most homes in this shattered village looked the same.

'Pananas!' Ky jumped as Tem materialised behind him, the greeting spearing through his tender head.

176

'Bananas Tem. Good to see you.'

'Thought I'd lend a hand. Wyka and I just finished another house and I felt like a change of scene.'

'Great. It's always a bit tricky checking them out.'

'Ha. You never know what's inside, do you?' Tem moved closer, peering into the gloom.

Ky made out an abandoned bench and some angular chairs. Someone had carved them with an intricate weave of leaves and fabulous flyers.

'They'll want those lovely chairs back.'

Taking a breath, he stepped in further, untangling the legs from the surrounding mess. He floated them out the door.

'Someone there will recognise them.' Tem pinged them over to the hill to the new building site. 'Want me to come inside?'

Ky glanced outside into the brightness, tugging his ear. His mrug swooped down to follow the chairs, looping around them.

'It's good to have a lookout out there, in case a tmeg comes.' Ky turned back into the shadows.

'Only a tmeg?' Tem chuckled.

Ky pushed a table that leaned on three legs.

'Or eels. This top might be re-usable.' He sent that outside too.

Walking further into the gloom, he found a door at the back. As he pushed it open, something flapped madly on the floor. All the hair stood up on his head.

'Something's here.' He squawked. A dart of pain blasted through him.

'Ha. Eels? It's not flooded.' Tem joined him, eyeing his face.

As Ky's eyes adjusted to the dim light, he made out something moving, tangled in a blanket that had blown off the broken bed.

'It's just a spinner.' Tem climbed forward, grabbing the soggy corner. Slowly he tugged it away.

'I've seen a few about.' Ky didn't like to

admit he found them quite beautiful when the sunshine turned their spinning wings to rainbows.

Exposed, the spinner stared up at them. It had a bright expressive face, like a tiny earth monkey. It would have rested in the palm of his hand, but for the long wings on its back.

'Cute.' Tem froze, hands on hips.

Iridescent fur standing on end, it watched them with enormous pink eyes, shuffling its wings.

Gazing down, Ky felt a moment of connection, knew the clamouring hive mind attached. When they didn't move, he felt its burst of relief.

'It's-'

It leapt like an earth flea. The wings popped into a circle. It moved so fast he saw only a blur as it buzzed away out the gaping window.

'Good. Nothing else worth salvaging.' Tem stated, taking a last look around the bedroom. 'Let's go.'

They clambered back outside.

'Now for the hard stuff. Moving the whole roof is gonna take two of us.'

They stood in the overgrown garden, surrounded by nodding flowers.

Ky focused all his talent on the roof, winding up his power. The timbers began to rattle. The ground beneath his feet began to shake. He could feel Tem join with him, power swirling and crackling between them.

Bracing his feet, sweat beading on his forehead, he pushed up. Screams and cracks came from the breaking joints.

'Maybe we should take it apart,' Tem gasped through gritted teeth.

'Easier to re-use it whole. This should be simple.' Frowning, Ky fought the vibrations pulsing up his body.

The collapsed corner crumbled more stone.

The ground shook harder. Ky staggered, flailing his arms for balance.

Tem fell, groaning. 'This never happened

before,' he gasped, holding his knee. 'Look it's shaking the other homes down.'

Dancing, jaw clamped, Ky gave it one last push as the ground rocked beneath him.

Tem's power blinked out, exhausted.

The roof came free. It shot up into the air so fast the mrug had to dive out the way.

Dropping to his knees, Ky sent the roof over the hill. Closing his eyes, hands braced in the dirt, he rode the bucking ground. The mrug gave him a clear view of the roof settling down in the far field.

With a bang like a thunderclap, the garden leapt one last time, flinging him forward onto his stomach, his mouth full of blossom.

The bouncing stopped. Close by, a tree groaned and tilted. One of the houses collapsed sending up a cloud of dust.

Flipping onto his back, panting, he sneezed. The mrug circled high above as he spat petals.

'Weird.' Tem scratched his head. 'Maybe

it was us. More likely it was a quake.'

When finally he could breathe again, the dust descended. Ky sat up, coughing. The shaking did not return.

'Could we really have...? Nah.' Ky laughed.

'Who knows? C'mon, let's get on.' Tem stood.

Frowning, Ky returned to work, breaking down one crumbling wall. As it fell, the mrug swooped beneath, playing its usual game of dare.

'Go away. You'll get hurt,' Ky hissed. As usual it ignored him.

Tem felled another, sending them over to the stone pile on the new site.

Through his mrug's eyes Ky saw the trail of debris from the roof, the stones landing, sending up fat puffs of dust.

'Where are the electricity windmills?' Ky wondered, keeping one ear out for flyersong. He smiled, remembering those Dad put on the roof at home on Earth, with their eternal hum. No-one else in the village had anything like it.

'That's always the first job. Precious they are, since we developed washing machines.' Tem grunted as he hefted a large stone. 'Why you so worried about tmegs and eels?'

'A tmeg smashed up my cabin.' Ky shuddered, pinging wall logs to his timber pile. His head throbbed.

'It happens.' Tem grunted again, kicking down a corner. 'Don't get too hung up on it.'

'But I hear them coming.' Ky yanked more logs out, feeling his muscles ache.

'Ha. You can't miss a tmeg coming, can you?' Tem sent a heap of stone flying away.

'I hear the eels.' Ky whispered chewing his cheek. Wrapping his fingers around another log, he heaved. The strain felt good. Maybe he shouldn't have said anything.

'In water? Really?' Tem straightened, staring.

'They seem to be after me.' Ky nodded, rolling off another log that thumped into the dirt.

'Ha. Don't get so worried. It can't be

personal.' Tem crossed to another corner, triggering an avalanche of crumbling stones.

'Feels personal,' Ky growled, kicking a rock out the way, rubbing his temple.

He curled his fingers around another pole, feeling his back muscles take the strain.

'What are you doing?' Tem stared at him,

'Oh. I forgot.' Ky realised he'd been wrestling logs instead of pinging them. His ears burnt.

'Ha. Forgot.' Tem chuckled, shaking his head.

Finally looking around, Ky noticed a jagged crack in the ground snaking away from the house.

'Did we do that?' He grinned.

'Something did. I'll report that, now we're done. I'd better get back. See you soon, Ky.' Tem vanished.

The mrug settled to the ground beside him.

'What? You want me to try riding again? I'm very tired and not really in the mood.

Anyway, you hated it before.' Ky stared, dubious into the scarlet eyes. He rubbed his sore temple.

The mrug sent a wave along the edge of its wings.

'Is that a nod?' He fought the trickle of excitement sliding down his spine.

The mrug stared at him, rolling its eyes, waiting. Perhaps he was just due for another beating.

'Well, alright. Don't say I didn't warn you...'

Wrapping his fists around the base of the fat tentacles, he settled gingerly onto the mrug's back.

Its huge scarlet eyes flicked up at him. A burst of warmth spread into his brain.

Huffing, he braced himself, waiting for the deluge of fright and crushing distress from before.

The mrug broadcast waves of reassurance. Slowly it began to hover above the grass.

'Hey, this is fun.' Ky grinned, hanging on

tight.

In a flash, it slid away, as if the air were made of ice.

Clinging on hard, wind slamming his eyes closed, Ky gave a cracked whoop.

They soared.

When he dared peek again, spangling sea spread into the distance. The horizon was a curve of unfamiliar land far away.

'Wahoo. Amazing!' His yell was lost to the wind. He couldn't feel his tight-clenched fingers, nor his headache.

The mrug tilted, turning back.

'Hey!' Ky began to slide. A wing tipped up, pushing him back to safety.

Gulping, he looked back to the remains of the village.

That crack looked like an ominous scar. It zipped away into the distance.

Far away, a narrow stream of darkness drifted up into a swirl of purple cloud.

He frowned, catching sight of Fyl's team on their mrugs, escorting alongside in neat formation.

'Pananas, Ky.' Fyl waved. 'Mrugs talk, you know.'

Grinning, breathless, he nodded, afraid to let go.

After a while, the mrug seemed to feel him relax. It tipped its wings, dipped and circled. Another whoop emerged whole.

'Fay! I can really fly!'

'No need to shout!' He felt her wince, miles away.

'Sorry, it's just so...wow! Wahoo!'

The delighted mrug dived. Well balanced and gripping hard he was in control. Wasn't he?

Behind him, the team followed, shouting. He laughed.

They swooped down toward the trees.

One second they were in clear air, the next the mrug was plunging through branches, diving and twisting.

The boys yelled warnings behind him, too late.

Jaw clenched, Ky managed to hang on until a broken branch swept him off its back. He crashed to the ground.

Sprawling, winded, he listened to the slapping crunches as the mrug collided and fell.

'Ky?'

Above him, he could hear the boys calling out but for now he had no breath to reply.

He could only wait, gasping, feeling his ears burn, his lips stretched wide in a mammoth grin.

28

┊Chaos┊

Smiling, Fay thought of Ky as she returned to work after a long session with the grumpy narth that had required every healer. She couldn't wait to hear how his flying went.

Fay left the other healers, recharged with bread, ready for her next patient.

Myn walked in, her kittle wrapped tight in her arms.

Watching, the pale mrug squeezed her

leg, eyes shining.

'Pananas, Myn. Something wrong?'

'It's Fry. I can't keep him warm. We knitted him lots of jumpers but the threads stick in his blisters and he bites them off. I don't know what else to do!' The child tailed off with a wail.

'Have you been putting the cream on his wounds like I showed you?' Fay sighed.

'Yes. Exactly how you showed me.' Myn straightened from her slump.

'You know, you wouldn't have been here if you'd looked after him properly. I hardly recognised him when he came in, and now this...' scolded Fay, shaking her head.

'I know. I just couldn't catch him.' Myn's voice caught. Her sad eyes grew huge. 'But now he seems glad to come to me for the cream.' A smile broke through.

'Good. Well, have you tried altering something thin, like a tunic rather than hot knitting? Maybe it's too itchy for him.' Fay shrugged, frowning as Myn released her bald pet to prowl the room. 'Let me just take a look.' She snatched it up. The kitt yowled and spat, dangling upside-down.

Holding tight to its feet she checked the length of its legs, the bony body. The blisters were slowly healing. The skin didn't look so angry. She let it go.

It put its nose-slit toward the ground, sniffing.

'It's doing fine, Myn. Good job.' Fay nodded.

Myn beamed, reaching out to stroke her straight hair with wondering fingers.

'I think it's just embarrassed.' Fay shifted away, flicking her hair over her shoulder.

'Embarrassed?' Myn gasped.

'Well, how would you like having to walk around naked?' Fay grinned. 'All the other kittles have thick coats of fur.'

'Where'd it go?' Myn jumped off her chair. The kitt was nowhere to be seen.

Their eyes met.

'Oh no!' Together they leapt out into the

corridor.

'You go that way, I'll go this.' Fay pointed.

They split up, at a run. The mrug slid down her leg, giving her a limp.

The sound of chaos told her where to go.

⋮

Fay chased it, eventually, to her room. The silvery cape from the gaut mocked her from the hook on the wall. So much for forgetting.

'Found Fry.' She broadcast, showing where she was.

Myn came pounding down the hallway. Flushed, she leaned into the doorway.

'I think it just sorted its problem.' Myn pointed to the cape, giggling.

Nodding, Fay grinned. The kittle had wrapped itself in the gaut cape, tongue lolling, legs dangling.

'Ha. Really?' Shrugging, Fay snorted.

The gaut had told her someone needed it. At least she wouldn't have to hunt around for its new owner.

'Well Myn, it seems to know that's what it needs. Good luck with sewing that to fit.'

She unhooked the cape, kitt still wrapped inside. The silvery weight of it seemed to glow with warmth. The old gaut's face drifted before her eyes. 'It seems to be working already.'

'What is it?' Wrinkling her nose, Myn took the kittle back in its new wrapping. 'It smells fishy.'

'Does it matter, so long as it works?' Fay shrugged, casual. The girl didn't need to know.

Myn eyed her, dubious. 'Well, Bostril, Fay. Thanks.'

'No problem. Now I have work to do. Enjoy your stitching.' Fay sent her off with a wave.

She chewed her lip as she turned back into the room.

Why would the cape of a dead gaut be so important to a kittle, and what of the spirit within it?

29

⫶Team⫶

The mrugs soared up into the sunrise sky. Fyl rode to his left. The rest of the team were spread out behind.

'Wahoo! I was never in a team before,' yelled Ky, trying to grin as the wind flapped his lips. A little sleep made him feel much better.

'Welcome. I'm Tytuth.' Called a lisping voice from behind. 'We have to be up early to patrol before we go to work. Thometimeth ith hard, but this taketh thome beating.' His grin revealed a missing tooth. A long, single plait flapped behind.

Glancing back at Fyl, he nodded towards the kaleidoscope sky.

To his far left, a late hunting flitter made a spidery silhouette above the trees, surrounded by a blizzard of fleeing flyers.

Down to his right a lumpy umbo plodded along a misty riverbank, snuffling for breakfast.

'So what are we looking for?' he shouted, clamping his teeth as the wind slammed at his eyes.

'Helps to wear a mask or cloth. I'm Byran.' Shouted the waving boy with a scarf tied around his narrow head, flattening large ears.

'I'm Snyz. Don't lean too far,' holllered another chunky boy rolling a flip behind Byran. A mop of dark frizz flopped around his head.

Ky hastily straightened his back, facing forward again. The mrug's red eyes flicked up at him and away.

'Look out for injured creatures. Anything that needs help. Landslides or rock falls. Anything unusual or different.' Fyl swung an expansive arm.

'Am I supposed to know what's diff--?' Ky daren't let go the tendrils to scratch his head.

'Ha. You'll know.'

'I will?' Frowning, Ky squinted down as sunbeams began to pierce the sky.

'We have to check on the Sour Sea.'

He was higher than any mountain, higher than he'd ever been. It wasn't just the wind that stole his breath.

'Sour sea?' He couldn't look away from the rainbow sun's rays.

'Yes. We're coming to it now. Look.' Fyl pointed. Across a flat plain where desert reigned, something glinted, acid orange.

'What is it?' Ky squinted into the brightness.

'It's a sea of sour. I don't know the Earth word. Poison I suppose. Only a few creatures have adapted to live here and drink it. It stains them tangerine.' Fyl pointed as a lean creature, like a skinny badger striped rusty, scuttled into a burrow as their shadows passed.

'What's that?' Ky craned down, but it was gone.

'A sourpuss. It eats the crystals.'

'A sea of crystals.' Ky blinked, blinded by the glare reflecting off the shiny shoreline. No rocky shore here. Geometric lumps of amber glass, all shapes and shades, jutted all around the edge. A million mirrored facets flashed the sun. Some rose into elegant spires. Others had shattered to crumbs.

'The thea'th gone!' Tytus lisped, gasping behind them.

'It must have drained away. See, the crystals are all that's left. That spells trouble.' Fyl's mouth turned grim, circling.

'Let's get a closer look.' Snyz swooped

197

down to skim over the surface, Byran close behind.

'There's a crack! I can see it through the crystals. I'm following it.' He zipped away.

'Look.' Snyz yelled. 'Byran! Watch out!'

Ky saw Byran spin a tight circle, head whipping round. Beyond him, violet steam billowed out from the rocks above the empty sea.

'I saw it yesterday.' He spun around too, watching it roll and curl into the air.

'That's bad news. Let's go on!' Fyl barked.

'It comes from where the crack was leading.' Byran yelled, swooping up.

As one, they soared away.

'It's huge!' Ky marvelled as they followed the edge of the cloud for miles.

It roiled above the mustard beach by the jelly sea, raining down on the broken spaceship rusting on the shore. Everything beneath it was black. The metal of the ship smoked. It stank.

'That's the ship I rescued Dad from.

Nothing new there.'

'Metal thmoking like that, thomething'th theriouthly wrong.' Tytus shook his head, glum.

'I'd better report it quick.' Fyl shook his head, closing his eyes.

⁇

It wasn't like her to miss breakfast.

'Fay?' The window to her mind was closed. Perhaps she was busy early too. Shrugging, Ky tucked into his cereal with the team all around him. It felt like family. He just needed his parents there. They probably needed more time alone. Soon everything would be perfect.

He day-dreamed a golden future mapped out ahead. Every day would start with the squadron. What better way to start a day? After that, work and sometimes visits with family. The days would finish off with happy meals at Central Eating.

Depending on what happened with the cloud, of course. Such burning power could wreck the whole planet. He wriggled uneasy shoulders.

Since when had his dreams ever come true?

30

⋮Ruffle⋮

Myn appeared in her room. Eyeing Fay's angry face, she clutched Fry tighter.

'I'm sorry to follow you home.' Myn's round eyes begged for understanding.

'You shouldn't be here.' Fay snapped, rubbing weary temples.

Blinking fast, Myn stepped back into the hallway.

'I just so wanted to show you the coat we

made.' Beaming, she held out her pet.

Fay's bad mood instantly faded. The poor creature wore frilled pyjamas and a coat edged with more frills. They'd even covered its tail. To top it all, they'd made it a hat that looked like an old-fashioned bonnet. Its solitary lavender plume had a special hole to itself, sticking out the top like a feather.

'Oh.' She covered her mouth with a polite hand.

The gaut that donated that cape would have died of embarrassment, if it hadn't already.

'There's certainly a lot of work gone into that,' Fay croaked, squeezing away her grin.

'He's so much happier to have something smooth to wear,' Myn crooned.

Her pet gazed at Fay with a great, sad eye. It whined, pitifully.

'It's strange stuff. Warm. We had terrible trouble sewing it.' Myn held out a ruffle. Fry rolled his eye.

'Better than being naked.' Fay, nipping

her lip, wasn't so sure.

'What did you say it was, this stuff?' Myn tipped her head.

'I didn't. Now if you don't mind, I need to sleep,' she lied, fighting down her grin.

'Oh. Well, we'll go then…' Myn turned away, head dipping down.

'Thank you for showing me,' Fay blurted, ready to kick herself.

'That's alright.' Myn's smile was back as she pinged away, waving her prisoner's bony claw.

⋮

Once the howling laughter receded, Fay went for a long stomp in the woods.

She would never sleep, not for hours now. Not that sleep was something she ever enjoyed.

Her pale mrug squeezed her shin.

'I don't mean to stand on you, you know. You're just getting big.' Looking down, she felt the need in its eyes.

'Oh. Again?' She prised it off and set it on

the ground, where it gushed into the weeds. She felt a stab of relief from it. It must have been waiting a while.

'I suppose we both needed to make an effort, eh?'

The mrug nuzzled her foot. As she wrapped it back round her leg, they shared a smile. Then she spotted her hand. The nails had turned a pearly shade of blue. She flexed the fingers, threading them through the straight hair over her shoulder. One hand, one side of her head.

'Neat.' Maybe she was changing into something else. She should talk to Wyka, the only expert on that subject.

She strode on, checking for clouds, stewing, losing track of time.

It wasn't until the world turned to fire around her that she realised she should no longer be outside.

The glow of Barus stained the world red, as the creatures' began their hunting frenzy. The air shook with their hungry roars. Time to go.

Pinging back to her loathsome bed, she stared at her nails in the light of the blimworm. If she wasn't changing, maybe there was something wrong with her.

Shuffling into a comfortable position, she expected to lie awake for hours. So many problems whirled round in her head.

As soon as she turned the blimworm off, her busy day caught her up, washing her away into the future.

31

:Sinking:

Patrolling early next morning, Ky and the squadron circled the lavender cloud. Even at a distance, the stench from it filled their lungs. It billowed from the crack, now twice the cloud it had been yesterday. The land beneath was not just in the shade, it was red as dried blood.

The mood over breakfast was sombre.

Even the mrug seemed subdued.

Ky, eager to escape the gloom, popped onto the treehouse deck, disturbing a cloud of spinners that flew up around his head. Lashing their tails at him, they made a rainbow blur. With a flip, his mrug swooped down, frightening them away.

As the last spinner clattered off, he sent the mrug to hunt.

Stepping toward the window, he gazed up at the live tree trunks holding up the porch.

Something wasn't right. Misery oozed down his back like treacle. Faintly, he could hear sobbing. His chest started to ache.

'Mum?' he called, following the sound.

He heard a snuffle as he rounded a corner, caught her dragging an arm beneath her nose.

She popped to her feet, running towards him.

'Ky! It's so good to see you!' She wrapped him in bony arms, hiding her face in his shoulder.

'You too.' He wished he'd brought a gift.

Before she arrived, he'd tried to pick her flowers. She'd never understand what it would cost him to pick them, denying their pain and protest. He couldn't bring himself to do it.

Ky wrapped her tight in his arms.

'You alright?'

'I am now.' She clung tight for a long time.

'Where's Dad?'

'He went. I dunno.' Her voice caught.

Ky scowled, feeling his ears burn. He shouldn't have to feel responsible for her any more.

'Um. I'm thirsty.' Ky wrestled away.

'Oh. Sure. Sorry.' Sniffing, she backed away, turning to the house as she spotted his eyes on her face. 'I brought coffee, your favourite.'

'Can I help?' He headed for the tap.

'I don't think I have a cup.' She spread out her hands, eyes glistening again.

'Oh. Well, we use mugs here. This'll do.' He gulped cold milky coffee, the scent flashing him back to France a lifetime ago.

'Great idea.' Her lip trembled.

'Are you okay, Mum? Do you have a headache?' He suddenly recognised the shadows and pallor in her face. 'We have herbs for that.'

'No, no. I'm fine.' She lied, not meeting his eyes. 'So come sit. Tell me where you've been, what you've been up to. We have a lot of catching up to do,' she gabbled, leading him into the lounge, which still smelled strongly of fresh cut wood, like the cabin.

'I've been flying.' Face burning, Ky pointed up the tree through the angled glass ceiling. His mrug zoomed above like a stealth jet. 'Mrugs are incredible! If you start to slide they just tip up a corner and push you back on.' He darted around the room, arms out, trying to demonstrate. 'Mum it's the best! It's like being on top of the world up there. I can see into forever.' He stopped to wave at the mrug, fighting the urge to ping himself up there.

'That's amazing. Sit. Sit.' She patted a cushion.

'I joined the squadron yesterday. Well, I did my first flight.' Ky sat, finally noticing a few of their things from home around the room. 'Every morning I'll be with them now.' He bounced in the seat.

'Where've you been?' She perched on the edge of a chair.

'We were patrolling,-'

'No, I mean where are you sleeping?' Mum shook her head. He stared, hurt.

'I'm well, still living in Jax and Dit's cabin. Would you like to come see it? I'm helping on the rebuild in the valley...'

'Your grandparents are so sweet. Everyone is.' Her voice caught again.

Ky eyed the gleam in her eyes.

'And I'm still doing all the studies with the other kids.' He continued, to fill the silence, cursing himself.

Frowning, he was soon bogged down,

trying to share what he'd had to learn on Mrax.

He scratched his head. It was hard to explain and he didn't want to frighten her. He'd forgotten there was so much he hadn't or couldn't tell her. Being so careful was hard work.

Besides, her experience would be different to his. She wouldn't have a tmeg after her. He glanced outside, just to check.

She kept rubbing her temples, something she didn't usually do.

He sucked his tongue, certain whatever he said would result in disaster.

It wasn't long before Ky found himself having to justify how he was making himself useful on Mrax.

'Of course I've heard of recycling!' She scoffed.

'Well, this is just the same, only for everything. We have to take things apart to rebuild. There's only so much material.'

'But that's just demolition.' She frowned.

211

'Your brain is better than that!'

'We only take down what's already broken. I can lift it with my mind and slot it where it's needed.'

Her eyes had glazed.

'It's just until I come of age here. I know Dit calls me a man but there are tests I have to pass first.'

'Pass? Oh, like exams. Then you can decide on a proper job. I see. Good.' She looked sick. Ky ground his teeth at her blind faith in Earth standards.

'Tell me about Fay.'

'She heals,' he tried.

'People? Animals?' She stared.

'Everything. Healing is healing.' He shrugged.

Gawping, horrified, she obviously didn't understand much of that either.

He was croaking now.

'Well, I,-'

'You need another drink.' She stood, interrupting him mid-sentence. The shadows were growing deeper around her face. 'Did you know we have our own mingo tree?' Here.' She handed him a jug of juice, bending to look at a shelf, or maybe hide her face.

'Cool. Thanks.' Frowning, he tipped some into his mug hoping the coffee dregs wouldn't curdle. What would she understand?

Gulping it down, he grinned.

'You're safe, in the cabin?' She grated.

'It's fine Mum.' He lied, feeling his ears burn. 'Look. I can tell there's something wrong. Tell me. Okay? Maybe I can help.'

He had a dark, sinking feeling that all his dreams were about to come tumbling down.

32

⋮Eclipse⋮

Awake early and grumpy, Fay pinged away from the clinic.

Without a plan, she found herself high on the hill above Ky's cabin. He was probably still asleep. Its fresh timbers stood out, stark against the trees.

She settled to a rock, drawing up her legs, stroking her straight hair, dragging knots from her curls.

Setting the mrug on the ground to explore, she sighed relief, rubbing her leg.

Resting her chin on her knees, she watched an eagle soar over the valley, its lonely call shivering down her spine. She spotted Ky's distinctive, scarred mrug, cruising in the distance.

It was a rare talent that she could merge with any creature. Fay didn't often use hers unless she was at work. It helped to calm or ease the pain. She envied Wyka's skill to become any creature she liked, an exceptional talent.

As the huge mrug drew nearer, curious, she connected to it, joining it to follow the eagle.

After the first rush of vertigo, she could see minute details all the way to the horizon.

'Wow.' Those red eyes really were special.

Then the mrug took off after a flyer. The images blurred with the speed. Its hunger burned down the connection like fire. She broke off, feeling cast adrift, in freefall, losing all concept of time. What seemed a moment later, she was back in her body, shaking on the rock.

The sun had leapt up the sky.

Jerking from her daydreaming state, blinking, she clambered to her feet.

Was it getting dark? Snapping her head up, she gazed at the sun. A black circle was sliding in front of it, blocking out the light.

The eclipse!

Below in the valley, creatures were roaring, hooting.

She jumped to her feet. Casting out, she felt sudden fear, violent anger, frenzy overtaking them.

A flitter, dancing on the air, made a dark silhouette, roaring.

Around her feet, the smallest creatures were biting each other as they scuttled to shelter.

Frowning, she looked around. Her mrug had vanished.

She'd missed previous eclipses before. It

was growing darker every minute. The uproar around them grew louder. Slithers began to wind through the undergrowth.

Hadn't Pa said the warning was for snow and death?

Frowning she looked up.

Without the sunshine, the temperature was dropping fast. Goosebumps broke out all over her.

In the valley, she saw fights breaking out, maddened creatures ripping into each other. She'd never seen anything like this. Their pain washed through her.

She summoned her mrug.

The ground shuddered beneath her.

A swirl of lilac cloud spiraled above, tinted red.

The screams below grew louder. Her stomach clenched.

Crunch! She turned to see a narth approaching on the path, tail straight up like a flagpole. Steam rose from its great hump of back, gushed from its nostrils. Thick,

217

speckled pink flesh juddered with every step.

Her heart began to thump. Creeping forwards, her pale mrug emerged from beneath a bush.

The narth's angry little eyes inspected her as the tree-trunk legs stomped closer. It snorted its piggy nose.

Its breath blew over her, rank and hot.

The cloud spun nearer, darker.

She began to shake, eyes flicking between the narth and her mrug.

The first frozen drip off the approaching cloud drifted down. It landed on her arm, stinging. She didn't dare look.

More flakes hit the narth.

It jumped at the first one, snorting.

As more fell, it began to twitch and dance, glaring down at her, huffing.

The ground trembled again. She threw out her arms for balance.

The mrug was edging closer, too slow.

A second flake stung her arm.

The narth charged, skipping and

squealing as more flakes struck.

'Come on!'

The mrug crept forward, gazing up at her. She wound up her power.

The ground bucked. She staggered. A thunderous ripping sound cracked the air. A step rose in the path.

The leaping narth tripped, smashing to the ground, sliding towards her.

'Oh no.' That grinding sound would haunt her dreams.

Trees folded out the way, mud spouted.

Finally, its huge snout came to rest at her feet, gushing foul breath.

Frozen too close, she watched another purple flake land on its skin, watched it dissolve into black. The skin began blistering, bubbling at the spot.

The narth growled, narrowing its mean little eyes. She saw the muscles work in its jaw, its shoulders. It was ready to leap again.

The ground beneath her began to judder, dark snow hazing her view. Lurching, she began to fall.

Dodging that snapping mouth, as the ground opened up, she lunged for the mrug, pinging them away.

33

⋮Torn⋮

Ky's mother leapt off the chair, pacing the room.

'It's nothing. Just a down day. You know.' She shrugged, as far across the room as she could go. She hugged herself, gazing out into the clustering trees. A cloud passed over the sun.

Ky gazed at her silhouette, scowling. It was growing darker by the minute.

'No I don't know.' He crossed the room. 'Mum... Is it Dad? Has something happened?'

'No! Dad's fine. We're fine. He's just so busy.' Her fingers clenched on her ribs. 'Don't worry about it.'

Ky ground his teeth.

The Ancients wouldn't listen to him, probably wouldn't understand.

His father was torn both ways, caring for Mum yet catering to the endless demands of the Ancients, as he had done all his long life.

He needed to change things for them. So what could he do?

His thoughts jerked back as his dad returned, apologising for his delay. Ky scowled at him.

His mum lit up.

Wrapping an arm around her, Balzar stared into her face.

'You look as if you have a headache.' Touching her cheek, he glared at Ky, like it was his fault. Maybe he was picking up all the unhappy vibes too.

'Just tired and hungry,' She shrugged, looking away.

'Me too,' Ky croaked, eager to escape. She didn't need him now.

'It's much too early,' Balzar stated, looking outside with a frown. 'How about I make you some tea? Didn't we bring some biscuits?'

'Can't go out during an eclipse.' Dad's eyes caught Ky's as he stood.

'Why?' Ky frowned at his father's back.

'Listen.' Balzar fussed by the sink.

Ky's eyes flicked to the window.

An eerie darkness had settled. A black circle rode high in the charcoal sky, ringed with bright light.

The flyers had stopped singing. In the thick silence, roars and squeals rang loud. A scream close by chilled his blood.

'Let's have some music from home, eh?' Ky fumbled out his phone and found an album to play. He turned the volume up.

'Good idea.' Balzar's voice in his head

223

brought Ky a little glow.

Too late, he looked back at his mother. All the colour had drained from her face. Dark pits hung beneath her eyes. Her lips trembled as her eyes flicked between them.

'Why is it dark?' Her voice twanged, tight as violin strings.

'It's just an eclipse.' Shrugging, Balzar offered her the packet of biscuits. 'We have four moons so they happen more than you're used to.'

'Oh.' Slowly she raised a shaky hand to take one.

'I love this track.' Ky slapped the rhythm loud on the arm of his chair to drown out the rising din.

Roaring, something crashed into one root-strengthened corner, sending down a shower of leaves. Scrabbling high against the glass roof set Mum quivering.

'Wh-what is that?' she whispered, staring up at the dark shadow above.

Ky gulped, meeting his Dad's eyes as he

set down the tea. He could feel the tingle of his father's power spiralling up.

'Just a flitter Mum.' Ky replied, catching a glimpse of wing and a slashing, hooked leg. At least the darkness concealed its size and details of the fight.

Mum's biscuit was showering crumbs everywhere, clenched in her white knuckles.

Balzar took Mum's trembling hands in his, staring into her eyes.

'I told you before, you're safe in here. It's just the eclipse. Sends them crazy for a while. But it won't last long. Then they'll all go sleep it off and peace will return. Drink.' He prised open her hand to deliver the mug.

Ky felt the surge of his power. Helping his father, they dumped the flitters down in the valley, where they could be crazy as they liked.

'See?' Balzar met his eyes, nodding slightly.

Ky's track ended and a new tune came on, starting 'I see monsters.' Quickly he fumbled for another track with a heavy beat.

She sipped her tea, wide eyes staring intent at the roof, out through the windows to the deck. The thumping tune didn't stop all ears from straining.

A fire squirrel fleeing above made her jump.

'Oh no. It's all over me.' She wailed, dabbing at her jeans. 'I'll just go change.'

She jumped up without meeting their eyes, scuttling into the bedroom.

Ky shared a grim glance with his father, who nodded at the window. A vast, dark shape blocked the view, then vanished. The roof was black with a wave of passing slithers. The outside corner roots were knotted up in them.

'You shouldn't have left her.' Ky hissed, unable to hold back any more.

A shudder seemed to go through his seat. He looked back, but the creature was gone.

'The Ancients-'

'It's always them! Time and again you let

us down to run to them.' He snapped. 'It has to stop, Dad.'

'But I-'

'No excuses Dad. Either you want her here or you don't. It's bad enough you're always letting me down. Now you're doing it to her.' He snapped his teeth, as his fist hit wood. His face and ears burned from the boiling in his veins.

Balzar gawped.

The shiver came again, trembling through his toes, shaking down leaves. Maybe it was rage.

Across the room his father frowned at the sound of soft footsteps. He shook his head at Ky.

'That's better.' Mum returned, settling back to her seat. Picking up the remains of her tea she looked from father to son, tucking her hair behind her ear.

'What is it?' Perhaps she could feel the tension. Maybe he was beet red.

'Look.' Ky pointed at the semi-circle sun.

227

'It's going. The light's coming back.'

Outside, the shrieking waned. Ky let the track finish, turned the phone off. Time seemed to have slid away like a slick. The silence felt wonderful, if slightly electric.

'Finish your tea. Then, I guess we can introduce you to the delights of Central Eating.' Balzar grinned, as if nothing had happened.

Mum took one last look outside, as the world returned to normal.

'I'm glad that's over.' Suddenly, she sounded stronger. 'Right I'll go find my jacket.' She popped up from her seat.

Gazing after her, Dad's eyes shone red with distress. Good.

'How often does the eclipse happen?' Ky met his father's eyes, changing the subject, so he wouldn't scream at him.

'Not for ages and then there's a lot. Boyng thinks we're in for many, soon.'

'And the tremor?' Ky felt his face cool. He unclenched his fists.

'*So slight she didn't notice. Let's just hope it's not the start of something bigger.*' Dad scowled, rubbing his temple.

'*Don't want to think about it. Will there be any food out at Central Eating so quick?*' Ky gazed out the bubble window.

'*We may have to wait.*' His father shrugged.

'I'm ready.' Mum smiled. 'Oh, I forgot to brush my hair.'

'You look beautiful.' Balzar's soft smile was reflected on her lips.

Ky rolled his eyes.

'I'll be quick.' She shot away, returning looking just the same. The familiar routine seemed to have soothed her.

'Right. Let's go then.' Balzar touched her cheek, twining her fingers with his.

Sighing Ky was glad to ping away.

The effects of pinging made her legs buckle again. She clung to Dad for a while, pale but soon smiling at his teasing.

She would not realise that the cook fires

had only just been lit or that food was still arriving from storage.

Safe in his father's arms she didn't seem aware of much at all.

Ky couldn't help scanning the trees for any sign of movement. He watched the griddles fill, delicious scent billowing into the air. By the time Balzar had filled her bowl and reintroduced her to Fay's parents, Voyn and Dylys, she was chatting, lively. Colour returned to her cheeks.

Fay settled with her family on a nearby bench, winking at him.

'Have you set Ky on the path to his coming of age?' Dylys asked, beaming at Fay.

'What does that involve?' Mum leaned forward, eyes bright.

'Ah, well, it's complicated...' Voyn put in, rubbing his hands. 'There are various elements to complete, to prove they can take their place in the adult world. Challenges, if you like...'

Ky and Fay shared a mental groan as he

launched into a monologue. Eventually, Dylys gave him a shove.

'You're boring them, dear. I'm so sorry. Finish your food, Voyn.'

Ky suddenly became aware that he was squinting. It had turned dim again. He looked up.

A second eclipse was stealing the light. His heart began to thud. So soon?

A hush fell over the meagre, early crowd.

'This is wonderful. Delicious!' Mum gushed in a high voice. 'I didn't know you had lobsters!'

Others in the shelter stopped chewing to stare at her.

'Sealouse.' The word drifted into his head. Fay winked. *'Stranded on a storm tide.'* Ky snorted, choking on another juicy chunk.

Scanning around, everyone shovelled their food fast, keen to escape, including Ky and Balzar. The slithers would be back any moment.

His mother was savouring every

mouthful.

'I've never seen her like this. Is she alright?' Behind her, ready to ping away, Fay made winding motions with her hands, rolling her eyes.

'Stressed I think.' Ky replied. *'It's all so new and strange for her. The eclipses aren't helping.'*

Mum probably just thought it was evening. Two eclipses so close never happened back on Earth.

Voyn and Dylys made polite excuses and left. Fay lingered, chewing her finger, trying to feed her mrug.

'You don't need to stay, Fay. We can deal with this. But thanks for the moral support. Be safe. We'll catch up tomorrow.' He nodded at her, scanning the trees for tell-tale spikes.

Balzar kept meeting Ky's eyes as his Mum asked what each vegetable was. It became more of a guessing game, as darkness settled over them.

'Blue bread? Oh, it's lovely. What's in it?'

If only she'd just shut up! Ky grew acutely aware of the tension around them.

'Hurry up and take her home!' Fay vanished, waving impatient hands.

Everyone else had gone. Growls rumbled deep from the gloom.

Ky used his sleeve to swipe away the sweat beading on his forehead.

'You leave a crust for last and wipe the bowl. I can see why you would. Shame to waste even a drop.'

Mum didn't stop chattering until the screaming drifted in close on the wind.

'What is that?' She asked carefully, finally setting down her empty bowl. Ky noticed her hand shook, like his. About time.

'I think the creatures are upset by the eclipse.' Balzar replied carefully, standing. 'I think we would be wise to go home now.'

'Another one?' Mum croaked, squinting up at it.

The ground beneath them trembled. Gulping, Ky scanned the trees for spikes. On a distant hill he glimpsed a tree fall.

'Yes. Let's go.' Balzar took her arm. The first slither emerged from the trees, hungry head held high, mouth agape.

'I think I'll go to bed now too.' Kissing his mother, nodding to Dad, Ky took his moment to escape. 'See you soon.'

Home, he kept anxious watch out the cabin window for hours that night, not ready to ping down to the cave. The tremors continued, shaking the edge of his cliff away.

Knots of slithers passed by, chasing slinkers. Some even climbed over the roof but nothing came inside.

With the second eclipse gone, and the shuddering in the ground finally stilled, Ky convinced himself that all was well, until he tried to close his eyes.

34

⋮Jolt⋮

Groggy, Fay struggled out of her tangled covers, hooking up her blimworm. Her heart thumped, nightmares still dancing behind her eyelids.

Exhaustion had snatched her away, released her, then snatched her back, time and again. A procession of shocking images still floated in her head. It really could not be described as sleep.

Her arm hurt. Looking down, she found two burn holes in her arm. The snowflakes!

Jumping into her clothes, she went to wash. The water stung on the burns. She found some herb paste, smearing it on thick. Wincing, she bandaged her arm with an old tunic. She'd worry about that later.

Emerging, she found the corridors empty. It must still be really early. She wished she could see the sunrise from her room.

Why not? She dragged on several layers for warmth and pinged.

$$\vdots$$

The tallest mountain, Panchak had to be the best place to see the deadly cloud.

It loomed on the horizon, stretching far further now than it had when she'd first seen it in her dream. Burnished edges rolled and boiled into towers in the sky from enormous trenches where the land had sunk.

Faintly, she picked up its chemical stench, wrinkling her nose.

She pinged to a closer peak. Now she could see the result of the quakes, the trail of death the cloud left, of skeletons and ash. She felt sick.

A flock of birds tracked its edge, dark specks cruising in the far distance. As they curved towards her, she suddenly realised they weren't birds at all, they had corners. It was the squadron, equally concerned about this threat.

Her sore arm throbbed beneath the bandage.

Somehow, they had to stop it.

⋮

Arriving back at the clinic, she immediately set to work, healing a succession of new burns similar to her own, most of them far worse.

Injuries from the poison cloud were becoming all too familiar. The day passed in a weary haze.

'Take this, with my thanks. It's a very

special clip.' Something hard slid into her palm, as the final patient pinged away. Bleary, she shoved it in her pocket, plodding to the healer's rest room, rubbing her throbbing arm.

'If we don't stop this cloud, it'll be the end of the world.' Grim beside her, Eryl, the senior healer, shook her shaved, ornate head.

'I saw it this morning, gushing from cracks left by the quakes.' Fay nodded, weary.

'I've reported it.' Eryl nodded, offering her a chunk of bread.

Fay winced as she reached for it.

'What's wrong with that?' Eryl asked, catching her arm.

'Same as everyone we just healed.' Grabbing another handful of bread, she sank onto a bench, leaning her aching head back against the rock wall.

'Here.' Eryl settled beside her, closing her large eyes.

Sacred warmth grew under her hands. Fay had always healed others, she'd never felt that healing touch herself before. She smiled.

'Ahh. Thanks.' Fay sighed relief, chewing.

The clip in her trouser pocket dug into her leg. She pulled it out, staring down at the painted trumpet flower. She lost her appetite.

'This will only get worse, won't it?'

⁞

'I brought your breakfast, snoozeball. Again.' Fay popped her head around the cabin door. 'You missed your mum, too. You look awful.' She frowned.

'Can't sleep. Just lie there all night listening. By morning I'm a zombie. Still, I went with the squadron again, earlier. Then I must have crashed. That cloud's growing.' Ky rubbed his bloodshot eyes, sitting up on his tangled bed.

'What you need is food and fun.' She pushed the loaded shell into his hand.

'I'll just move some-'

'Nope. Let that wait.'

'You don't.' He glared, cheeks stuffed with food.

'Mine can be life or death. Yours is building. Tem can work a bit extra for a change.'

'But-'

'Fun. Fancy skiing again?'

Ky grinned, the slice of red fruit set over his teeth a good match for his eyes.

⋮

Skiing a strange slope with different pitfalls had been a bad idea. Fay grimaced, sliding behind as, gliding a tricky curve, Ky lost control.

'Aah!' Sliding into a crack in the hillside, he vanished.

'Ky!' Heart thumping, Fay pinged down to join him in the gloom, so close she fell over him. 'Oops. You okay?'

Scanning around the cave as she recovered her balance, Fay spotted the crack he'd fallen through, a stripe of light far above.

'I'll live.' He rolled his shoulder.

'Let me— Ooh. There's a webber in here. I feel it.' Fay quavered as she tried to focus on it.

'How big?' Ky breathed, rubbing his bruises.

'This is no ordinary webber.' she trembled.

'Why?'

'It's ancient. Oh no, it's a stabwebber!' she hissed, shaking.

'Like the hatchling in the safe cave? Does that mean-,' Ky whispered.

'Yup. But it's huge. And I can feel it's very hungry.' Peering into the dark, Fay's hands began to shake.

'When you say huge...' Ky cupped his hands making a shape big as a beach ball, raising an eyebrow.

'No Ky. I mean massive: Bigger than a double-decker bus with four sets of giant lobster claws and three lethal stingers.' She huffed, eyes flicking back up to the crack.

'And it's hungry. Which means we're um, on the menu?' Ky's mouth twisted. 'But it's a webber right? So if we don't get caught in the web, we're alright. Aren't we?' He peered around.

'Apart from the claws and stabbers,' Fay hissed, staring at him.

'Can't see it. Maybe that's what smells of old socks.' Ky tugged his ear.

'I'd be surprised if we do see it.' Fay mumbled, all the saliva drying up in her mouth. 'I smell cheesy vinegar.'

'See those tiny lights dancing up there?' Ky took a further slow, grinding step.

'Maybe that's how it sees its prey.' Fay shuddered.

'Got a blimworm?' His feet crunched forward.

'I wish.' She breathed.

Digging out his abused phone, he shone his torchlight all around. Shadows seemed to swirl around their feet.

'Slinkers are coming.' Fay gasped,

panther hunger flooding through her.

'What are these tall columns?' Ky frowned, craning to see where they soared up into the darkness.

'Columns?' Fay husked, clutching his cold hand.

'Columns aren't usually hairy, are they?' He croaked, shaking.

A clacking sound sent their eyes peering up into the darkness. More tiny lights jiggled up there.

His gulp sounded loud in the silence.

'Time to go, I think.' decided Fay. The air around her crackled as she wound up to ping.

'I just want to see...' Ky's voice cut off at a snapping like castanets.

Something stabbed into the ground by her foot.

A giant mouth, clattering with snipping pincers, fell towards Ky.

Grabbing his arm, screaming, she pinged them up and away as the slinkers burst into the tunnel.

35

⫶Fire⫶

Scratching, Ky discovered strange, moving dust stuck to his trousers the next morning. Whipping them in the cold, dawn wind to freshen them up, he shook off the lingering nightmare that had ended his sleepless night.

The squadron called for him, grim and quiet as they headed out.

'The stench from it's even worse,' grumbled Snyz

'It's still growing too. Byran gazed at the dawn sky filled with soaring marshmallow mountains in mauve and beige.

'More of the land'th thtained and burnt.' Tytus pointed at the haze of smoke.

They circled watching the cloud curl and roll, staring, helpless.

'What can we do against this?' Ky shivered.

'The Ancients need to see this.' Fyl snarled. 'Let's go.'

Ky was delighted to leave it behind.

⋮

Drooping, he closed gritty eyes, shifting enough timber to keep the builders below going for most of the day.

Taking breakfast, he visited Mum again, finding her hunched in a chair, miserable.

'So....' He urged, touching her shoulder. 'Are you homesick?'

She turned to face him, chin wobbling as he set down the shells.

'I guess there's some of that.' She

nodded. 'Dad's not here much and I miss my friends. What's wrong with your eyes?'

Ky frowned. Why hadn't Dad called him?

'I, I got some dust in them. There's nothing to say you can't pop home. Is there?' Ky yanked his ear, tasting bile.

'Balzar's so keen for me to love it here.' She sighed.

Something screeched out in the forest. She jumped, shaking. Her eyes popped wide.

'Dad should be here for you then.' Ky bit out.

'And if I can't go out, well I'm just a bit stir crazy....' She stared out the window, eyes welling.

'I can understand if you're scared. They're scary beasts, most of them.' Ky glanced into the shadows, watching for a glint of scales. Something huge seemed to move there in the forest gloom.

He shook his head. It was probably just his imagination, too many creatures haunting him lately.

Tugging his ear, his eyes flicked back to his mother.

'You can't ping away. I get that. So you shouldn't be alone...' He scowled. 'Has Dad thought about that?'

'Well, he wants us to be together but like I said, he's busy, keeps getting called away...' She trembled, eyeing the shaking trees.

Ky ground his teeth, shaking with rage.

As she turned, he caught sight of her livid hands.

'Mum your hands! What happened?'

'Well, I went outside to enjoy the view...'

'And?'

'I saw this lovely little squirrel. I'd never seen one so red before. It came closer, so I bent down to offer it the last of my biscuit...' She shuddered.

'Oh no.' Ky's eyebrows shot up.

'It was like it exploded. Fire shot over my hands. I yanked them back, ran in, held them under running water.' She gave a shaky laugh. 'When I looked up it was peeking in the window at me.'

'You should have been warned about those.' Ky followed behind, frowning as she vanished inside. 'Did you see a healer?'

'No. It's just scalds. I've been warned to avoid everything.' Her voice caught. 'So I don't go out now.'

'But that's crazy. You don't need this amazing house. You need people. Friends. And Dad or me, so you can be safe.' Ky nodded, clamping his lips.

'I've had tea with Dylys, you know, Fay's Mum. She's lovely. She said I could help the foraging team, but Dad doesn't want-'

'Dad's always helping out!' Snapped Ky, fizzing with anger. 'Believe me, I know how this feels. He did it to me too, always gone when the Ancients called. He promised. We need to make him think about it.'

'Oh Ky. You do understand! What should we do?' Her eyes gleamed with hope.

Gently, he took her cold, sore hands, feeling sick.

He had no choice.

'I think I should take you home for a while so he can do without you. See how he likes it.' Ky's plastic smile hurt his bitter face. 'That'll make him think.'

'Oh, I couldn't...' She tugged her hands away.

'I could. He needs to learn. Come on.'

Ky peered up at the mrug, sending it back to the cabin. It could fend for itself for the little while he'd be gone.

'Fay?' He sent but the window to her mind was closed.

'It'll be cold. Put on something warm.' He chewed his lip.

He'd only stay for a cup of tea. Then he'd ping right back, wouldn't he?

His stomach churned.

'But-,' She hesitated, shrugging into her jacket.

'Hey. We're going home.' He forced a smile, masking his sudden dart of dread.

Winding up his power, he sucked it from

249

the world around them.

At least nothing would be after him back on Earth.

So why were his sore eyes leaking?

Wrapping her in his arms, he pinged her back to Earth.

36

⁝Wink⁝

The last patient safely pinged back to its lair, the team retreated to their rest room. Fay fell upon the slugcheese seedbuns, ravenous.

The healers soon drifted wearily away.

Feeling her energy return, Fay wandered down the corridor, spotting a light in the supplies room.

'Pananas, Fyl. How do you do it?' She demanded from the doorway.

'What?' He looked up at her, fingers busy with another rope.

'Understand the mrug! Haven't had a dry leg for weeks!' The little creature sniffed, rolling its eyes.

'About time you did.' Fyl chortled, tutting as he dropped a thread.

'Well, I have a lot on my mind.' Fay defended, jutting her chin. One-eyed skeletons walked in her dreams too now.

'I know.' Fyl nodded, craning to look down at it where the mrug clung to her calf. 'Still, it's doing well. You just have to keep setting it down. It's getting big.'

'Mmm. I'm beginning to trip on it. Will I hurt it?' She rubbed its back with tender fingers, feeling it squeeze her leg.

'It'll learn to keep out the way.' Fyl shrugged 'Have you spoken to Ky?'

'He told me he could fly.' She nodded her head, hitching an eyebrow. 'Why?'

'He joined the squadron. Took his first ride.' Fyl grinned. 'He crashed, like all first timers, but we soon got him sorted out. He can be excused work for it now too.'

'Awesome.' Fay looked down at her mrug. 'Hurry up and grow.' She urged, tapping its nose.

It wriggled, winking one eye at her.

'Hey, it winked. Do they usually do that?'

'Perhaps it's trying to tell you something.' Fyl laughed.

'Now I'm worried. Oh.' She set it down on the floor.

'Look. It did it again!' A sizzle of excitement zipped down her spine.

'A mystery. Just like one of your dreams, eh?' Fyl smirked.

'Don't. Just don't, Fyl.' She scowled, shivering.

'Ha.' Fyl waggled his eyebrows.

'Well, it didn't want to pee.' Fay gathered up the mrug, wrapping it back around her leg. 'I have to go. See you later.'

Glowering, she pinged away.

⋮

Too early for dinner at Central Eating, Fay stomped into the woods. She wasn't hungry anyway.

She tugged her straight locks wondering if she had some awful disease. This mystery stuff was harder to deal with than she'd thought.

It was possible she was going through some kind of change.

Would her hair all fall out?

Maybe it was a warning.

As a healer, she should know. But if she didn't have a clue, who else could she ask?

She shivered.

Spinners chittered in the trees.

Flyers trilled.

Water trickled.

A spice breeze rushed through the leaves.

It reminded her of the sea. She sighed, remembering the gaut.

'Pa? Did you ask the Ancients about the

cloud?' She tried, combing through her long hair.

The window to his mind was still shut.

She ground her teeth.

Ancients would never be rushed.

She only hoped they decided what to do before it was too late.

37

⁞Home⁞

Mum's legs buckled as they landed in the garden. It was raining hard, loud. The crashing behind them merged with the ringing in Ky's exhausted ears.

Soaked and shivering, he swung an arm around her, heading for the back door.

He smiled to find the key under the flowerpot, as usual.

Awkward, he fumbled it into the lock.

They fell inside, draining puddles onto the floor.

She was pale, shaking. He set her on a chair, throwing down towels, wrapping one around her.

'Home.' She husked, with a feeble smile.

They both jumped at a rattle. A huge, dripping, cat stepped through a cat-flap he hadn't noticed in the door. Shaking its wet feet, it mewed and jumped onto his Mum's lap.

'I'm home, Puss.' Mum scratched its ear. It purred, circling, then settled on her lap. 'Well, I can't get much wetter.' She looked up at Ky. 'I got lonely.' Tears welled. Oh no.

'I'll make you a cup of tea. That'll make you feel better,' he whispered, keeping his trembling hands busy. 'I'm starving.'

Rummaging in the cupboards, he brought out a new pack of chocolate biscuits. The words on it swam.

Frowning, he saw them down a long tunnel, as if his eyes had telescoped out,

B. Random

darkness lapping at the edge of his vision. Something was very wrong.

'Ah. Chocolate. How I miss this.' Mouth watering, he fought the plastic. It took three attempts to break into the packet. Desperate, he stuffed two in his mouth at once. Grim, he chomped two more, yearning for his old bed upstairs.

At the centre of his tunnel vision, his mother just sat there, staring out the window at the rain. A droplet trickled down beside her nose.

The kettle boiled. Hanging on to consciousness, he forced his arm out to lift and pour. Hot water sloshed. The cups filled somehow. Slowly he replaced the kettle. His legs wobbled as he focused on mopping, the silence began to yawn, like him. Only the cat's purrs broke it.

'It's here,' she whispered.

'Huh?' Her words echoed round his empty skull. Like a toddler, he felt his way along the worktop to the fridge for the milk. Take it slow. One thing at a time.

The journey back from the fridge felt even longer. Ice seemed to be forming in his core, frost burning outward in his veins.

He flipped out the tea bags, slopping in the milk. The bottle rattled on the china.

He must need energy, fast. Two more biscuits disappeared into his mouth. He chewed, deliberate, desperate. His brain felt frozen. Gulping down the heat, tea showered his shirt. He slid Mum's cup toward her through the swamp he'd created.

She was still staring outside. Now her eyes bulged, her jaw sagged.

He stared at her, confused. His focus was shrinking, she seemed to be receding into the distance.

Before he could speak, the floor rushed up at him. The speck of light at the end of his tunnel faded.

He didn't hear her scream nor see the cat take off like a rocket.

38

⋮Weird⋮

In the light from the blimworm above, Fay dragged open scratchy eyes, yawning. Her dreams had been too confused to write down clearly. Just as well, she didn't feel she could lift a pen right now.

Every limb ached. Her joints cracked when she moved. Her head swam. Reality.

'Ky? She called into the void.

No response.

Ky's absence left a nagging itch at the back of her mind. No-one seemed to know what happened to him.

What if he'd been right about the tmeg being after him? No-one would know if it caught him. She should have listened.

Maybe he tried to tell her. Perhaps she'd been working. Maybe. Perhaps. Argh!

⋮

Outside, she was just chewing her final lunchtime tinga berry when Myn appeared, clutching her pet.

Just what I need, thought Fay, attempting a smile.

'Hi Myn. Fry looks very glum.' Fay bit her lip, staring into those sad eyes under the brim of the ridiculous bonnet.

'He keeps trying to run away. So I have to hold him even tighter.' Giggling, Myn squeezed her pet until its eyes bulged.

'Ooh. Gently Myn! This can't be good for either of you. Have you thought of a harness and lead?'

261

'We did try that. Pa made one for me, but when we tried to put it on over the clothes, it wouldn't stay done up. It was weird, like the material was sliding it off on purpose.' Myn shrugged.

'How strange.' Frowning, Fay flashed back to the dying gaut who'd said her spirit would go with it.

At the time she hadn't believed it.

'And I can't put it underneath. It doesn't have any hair yet and I'm afraid of hurting the blisters.' Myn waved the kittle's resisting paw. 'Fay's our bestest friend in't she?'

'Hmm. Shall I take a look at it?' Fay reached out.

Myn leaned forward. Fay caught her mrug under her foot staggering.

Somehow between them, the desperate kittle wriggled free.

With a frantic bounce it disappeared into the trees, hooting.

'Aww. Now I'll never find it.' Myn's huge eyes brimmed. 'I'll just die without Fry!' She flung a dramatic arm across her forehead.

Fay hid a grin.

'You're a poet and don't know it. 'Course you'll find it. You can hear it can't you?' Fay waved her hand.

'It's too fast.' Myn's tears overflowed.

Fay sighed.

'Come on.'

Grabbing Myn's hand she jogged off into the trees.

39

⁝Insane⁝

Rather than catch the school bus with his smug mother waving, just like his first day again, Ky pinged to a nearby corner, leaning behind a concealing fence.

It was bad enough that she couldn't bear for him to leave. She was always going to win; he just couldn't bear to see her cry.

He could have screamed when she'd

called the Head, determined. He'd shouted at her, couldn't help it. The anger still smouldered deep inside. But her eyes had filled up again and he was lost.

Besides, she was still so tense, staring constantly out the window. It probably hadn't helped, him passing out like that.

It shouldn't have been so exhausting. He'd pinged back many times now and never had that reaction. He chewed his cheek. Perhaps it was because he'd not been sleeping. He felt no better for his blackout.

Watching the stream of children pouring in, his feet itched to turn and run. It felt like rabbits hopped around in his stomach. Oh, for the freedom of Mrax!

When he'd lived here, he'd noticed the perfume of flowers, the scents of his food. He'd never considered how the normal, outside air smelled. Now he had something to compare it with. He wrinkled his nose.

A girl brushed past him, giving him a sideways look. She greeted a friend and the two of them whispered, peeking back at him.

Ky tugged his ear, huffing a breath. He should have cut his hair, should have bought new clothes. She hadn't given him time or money. Too late now.

He sniffed his armpit. Soap. Good. They wouldn't smell the fear.

No point putting it off.

Slouching in through the gates as the rain began, not meeting any eyes, he tugged down his tatty, too-small jacket.

'It's only for a little while, I promise.' Mum had said, fiddling with his too-small collar.

He gritted his teeth. She didn't understand. That was the problem. Never had, all those years when he'd told her he knew it all already.

He did want to see her happy again after all, he thought bitterly, watching his grubby trainers plod up the steps. She woke every night screaming with her nightmares, she said. Fay did that too, but she was used to it.

Yesterday, she'd woken him from

unconsciousness on the hard floor. Today every joint in his body ached. Even the cat was suffering this morning.

Stone turned to tile beneath his feet. Looking up, Ky realised he didn't know where to go. His last timetable would have been changed by now.

Stomach churning, he stopped by the lockers. Maybe he still had a key.

He swung off his backpack.

A shoulder barged him from the left. A tall boy with rampant zits and chin fluff gave him a dirty look. Reeling out the way, his phone flew out of his bag.

The boy swung his locker door open, just missing Ky's face. The attitude, at least, felt familiar.

Another shoulder barged him from the other side. Ky had to duck quick, so as not to smash into the open door. A second older boy eyed him with a sneer. Biting his lip, Ky failed to recall his name.

'Where d' you spring from?' he snarled, fat

lips peeling back, exposing his gums.

'I've just come back...' Ky mumbled, grabbing his phone before someone trod on it.

'Did you now? Well, that's my locker.' The boy shoved him away, into the flow of passing children.

'Oi!' Several hands shoved him back.

'Sorry. I'm looking for my key...' Ky stumbled to a doorway, hiding his hot face as he rummaged.

'Hey, look everyone! Ky's back!' yelled the second boy, gums gleaming, stuffing books into his pack.

Ky cringed, remembering how always being in trouble led to a dark kind of fame. The corridor fell silent. A hundred eager eyes turned to him.

'Hi.' He croaked, fleeing toward the Head's office.

The Head was just emerging, scratching his bald head. Ky leapt back out of his way.

'Ah. Ky. Back to try again? Good. I was

just coming to find you. Here's your timetable.' He thrust a sheet of paper into Ky's hands.

'Th-,' Ky was cut off by a loud burst of song down the corridor. The Head's mouth turned down. Laughter erupted. Before Ky could finish, the Head was steaming away.

Still safe in the little office hallway, Ky took a moment to check his cracked phone. It had come alive, colours streaming. He smiled. Shoving it safely away, he examined the timetable.

'Oh no.' A chill crept down his back.

A bell tolled his doom. The flow of children drained into the classrooms, unnoticed as he tried to slow his breathing.

He peered desperately toward the main door. The Head slammed it shut with a prison-door bang.

Gulping, he stomped off to music with the insane Miss Mimm.

Ky recalled how years ago he'd built himself a keyboard, after he'd mastered all

Dad's electronics lessons. It wasn't quite like the usual ones. He'd recorded animal and nature sounds, rhythmic horse farts, frog songs, tree creaks and lightning crackles, including them in his compositions. Previous music teachers commented that he had 'an unusual ear for sound.' Dad reckoned that was just a polite way to say they didn't understand.

Back then, Miss Mimm had rudely told him not to waste his time. Ky thought it was because he didn't try to fit her mould. She made no attempt to get to know him and never gave him a mark above F.

He stopped outside the soundproof music room door, peering through the little window. Already she was thumping her desk, coils of salt and pepper hair rolling like fat worms around her head.

The class all settled at their keyboards. She swung round, slicing lines, stabbing notes on the whiteboard. In profile her nose looked like an eagle's beak.

Reluctant, Ky pushed the door open a crack, allowing the sound of someone hitting a forbidden note to escape. Wincing at the flurry of sniggers, he silently drew the door shut again, watching.

Thick glasses askew, spittle flew as she shouted at her victim. The girl, pale as milk, stared down at the keyboard shaking as if it were a monochrome snake.

Mouth drying up, Ky rolled back against the wall. He'd be mad to go in there.

'Too good for lessons are you?' Sneered a familiar voice.

Ky looked up into the mean dark eyes of the second boy from the lockers. Gums. Whatever he said would be wrong. Sucking his tongue, he eyed the boy's prefect badge.

'Does anyone want to go to Miss Mimm's classes?' He tried a wobbly smile.

One cruel hand grabbed his collar. The other hand swung open the door.

'A pupil lurking outside, Miss Mimm.'

On tip-toe, Ky's too-small shirt drifted up

his chest, the hated tie strangling him.

The boy shoved him inside.

He straightened his spine, his shirt. For Mum, he'd set his life on Mrax aside for this temporary torture.

Tough if the teacher didn't like it.

40

⁝Swinging⁝

Fay tripped over the mrug again. Hours had passed. They were still stumbling along the path, watching the kittle swing through the branches high above.

It wasn't exactly camouflaged in those pyjamas; easy prey for any of the local predators.

'Oh no!' Myn croaked. 'Look, it's found some wild ones!'

'That's probably what it was looking for.' Puffing, Fay sank to a log, gazing up.

'Bet they're all asking where it gets its designer clothes,' Fay commented, concealing a grin behind her fingers.

The wild kittle family were all round it, sniffing and poking at the weird clothing. Hooting rose into a tune for just a moment, then reduced to whispers.

'Sounds like they're having a chat.' Myn smirked.

Their long arms reached out to Fry, touching and jerking back. One peeked underneath a frill.

'Ha. See?' Fay laughed.

Fry turned one huge eye to look down at Myn, or perhaps he was looking up at another kittle, it was hard to tell. It hooted three long notes.

The family, all legs, arms and fur, swung away rapidly into the trees. Silence resumed.

'It didn't go,' Myn whispered. 'I can't believe it.' A smile broke over her face.

'Call it,' Fay urged.

'Fry! Come to Ma. Come down Fry. Please.' Myn held out her arms.

Fry lay back against the trunk, crossing its long legs in their frilly pyjamas, swinging one burned, blackened foot. One giant, defiant eye stared down at Myn.

'Amazing. It wants to bargain, I reckon.' Fay snorted.

'What d'you mean?' Myn beckoned again.

'It means it's only coming back on its own terms, not yours.' Fay explained. 'Make a few suggestions, see what it wants.'

Probably freedom.

'How about an extra meal a day?' Myn yelled.

Fry just swung a leg, waiting.

'An extra blanket?' Myn shouted.

Fry didn't move.

'Try the suit,' Fay hissed.

'Okay. You can take off that suit. How about that?' Myn flipped a hand.

Fry just sat there, staring, intent,

wrapping its long arms around itself.

'You want a hug?' squawked Myn.

Fry unwrapped its arms, holding them out wide.

'I think it doesn't want you to hold it.' Fay grinned.

'Oh! But-' Myn's chin wobbled.

'You do hold it too tight Myn. Do you want it back or not?' Fay whispered.

'I won't hold you so tight. I promise.' Myn's eyes welled up.

Fry just stared, arms still wide.

'Okay. I won't hold you at all! But you have to stay with me and not run away or get into trouble again.' Tears gushing, Myn folded her arms. 'Final offer.'

Fry swung its leg once more. Sniffing, it began to clamber down the tree.

'I don't believe this.' Fay shook her head.

'Maybe Fry's special, a clever one.' Myn beamed. Dragging in a deep breath, she blotted her face with it, then snorted into the hem of her tunic.

Fry pranced towards them, pyjama frills flapping, tongue lolling.

Myn's arms rose automatically to cuddle him. Fry stopped, taking a wary step back. Sighing, Myn dropped her arms.

'C'mon then.' Turning, Myn ambled back down the path, glancing back at the kittle.

It began to bounce after her, bonnet bobbing.

'I think it's happy.' Fay laughed. 'Let's get moving, I'm supposed to be at work.'

⋮

For Fay, the remaining afternoon was short. They ran out of patients, so she was free.

She flopped on her bed with the mrug, wondering how she'd find the energy to ping to Central Eating, later.

'Ky?'

Frowning, she snuggled deeper into her covers. She hadn't dreamed anything bad happening to him last night. But there were plenty of awful possibilities in her book of dreams.

She sighed, feeling the deep icy throb where she'd drained all her energy. She was no use to anyone right now.

It couldn't hurt if she slipped into a long, long, doze. Could it?

41

⋮Alien⋮

It was the longest day of Ky's life. First he suffered the evil Miss Mimm followed by crazy Crockett for geography. Not much use to him on the wrong planet. Then came physics when he almost nodded off.

The rain continued outside, a deluge filling the worn patches in the field. Beneath the window, Ky watched a duck cruising down the edge of the roadway. Smiling, he thought of his mrug out there, splashing.

Then came break; the hardest time to stay out of trouble.

He hovered around the Head's office, pretending to be waiting, which kept everyone away.

Maths with Mrs Addison had filled the rest of the morning. He didn't hate maths. It was just too easy when you'd been doing quantum physics and star charts at seven with your dad. He'd learned a lot while Dad was around.

The hard part was keeping his mouth shut. So he continued staring outside, which had always earned him reports of 'not engaging in class.' He ground his teeth.

Outside, the shadows in the trees seemed to take on a definite shape. A shiver of unease skittered down his spine. No, this was Earth. His wild imagination was always triggered by the boredom.

He couldn't wait to leave. Doodling

himself in a tiny cage, fingers wrapped around the bars. It wasn't the same without Fay.

⋮

It was still raining at lunchtime. Chewing his cheek, he seriously considered pinging home from inside a toilet cubicle. But then he would have to deal with Mum.

He was slinking towards the cleaners' cupboard when someone swung him round.

'I heard you were back. Ha. It was a good name for you, bye-bye Ky.' Tate, his bully for years, laughed, copied as ever by his faithful side-kick Egan. Ky gulped, bitter memories flooding back.

Nothing had changed. Tate still had that stupid, biro spider tattoo on his neck. He'd added a few more here and there.

'Hi Tate,' mumbled Ky, jerking his shoulder away.

Expectant silence filled the corridor as passing students lingered to watch. A few hurried away, heads down.

Ky couldn't breathe.

'Now you do look like an alien.' Tate stood back to stare.

Automatically, Ky lifted a hand to cover the dark line down his neck.

'Have you come to take over? You gonna eat me?' Sneering, Tate leaned into his face. One stiff, vicious finger jabbed his stomach.

Grimacing, Ky folded, leaning out of range of his bad breath.

'Clear a path please.' Crazy Crockett coughed his way toward them.

'Ha. Take me to your leader!' chortled Tate under his breath.

'Get to your classes, students please, if you're not going outside.' Crockett flapped his hands, shooing the audience away. 'You too, boys.' His eyes flicked from Tate to Ky. He waited, hands on hips.

Ky glowered, unable to speak. Straightening, sore stomach churning, he hefted his pack.

Tate pretended to fumble for his locker key.

With a sniff, Crockett stalked away.

'Come here.' Ky croaked, tilting his head. 'I'll show you alien.'

Grinning, Tate stepped closer, jabbing finger ready. Egan closed in. Ky wound up his power, pinging them all up high, into the rain.

Shrieking, Egan fell away, thrashing. Tate was screaming too, spinning in freefall. The school was a postage stamp far below.

Rain drew silver stripes in the air, slicing icy through their shirts. Wind tore their hair up, stole their breath.

Shrieking, Egan was somersaulting over and over. Roaring, Tate thrashed into cartwheels. Ky flattened himself on the air, arms out, knees bent, waiting.

'Ky! Where are you?' Dad's angry voice came from far away. It was enough to distract him for one too many seconds.

They'd just passed the top of a pylon, when he grabbed their hands, pinging them safely down to the ground. Egan sprawled in a puddle, gagging. Tate's knees buckled too. He stared up at Ky, shaking. For once, he had nothing to say.

Turning up his face, Ky smiled, feeling the rain washing away the fear.

'Like that do you?' Ky stood over them for a moment, arms folded. 'Well, that's alien. So leave me alone. Next time I won't catch you.'

Turning he caught a hundred faces pressed against the windows. Dad would have to wait. Yanking his ear, sighing, he pinged back inside.

The uproar began as he was heading for the toilets to dry himself off.

Shouts grew behind him, ringing with familiar terror. Tmeg!

Dread twisting inside, he hurried back toward the windows.

Teachers were zipping in to join the crowd, craning over the children's heads.

Staring through the steamy panes, he realised his imagination had not been fooling him earlier.

The stabwebber was here, stumbling like a drunk across the field to where Tate and Egan were helping each other to stand. Steamy windows and slanting rain blurred the view but there was no mistaking it.

Relieved, he laughed. He wasn't going mad, imagining it.

Mum must have seen it when they arrived. She'd shrugged it off, as he had, thinking it was impossible.

Now the proof trundled across the grass, giant claws snapping, all three stabbers poised above like spears, dancing over the football goals that came less than half way up its legs.

Ky smiled to see Tate and Egan running.

'So this is funny, is it? Is this your doing?' The Head caught his arm.

Ky gulped.

'I don't know, sir.' He stepped away, shrugging off the hand.

It could have hitch-hiked back with him.

That would explain why it had taken so much of his strength.

'Do you know what that is?' the head hissed, leaning closer, trying to hide their conversation.

Some of the crowd were still glued to the windows, screaming. Others, wide-eyed, were fleeing.

'It's a stabwebber sir,' Ky whispered.

'It looks dangerous.' The Head's eyes drilled into him.

'Deadly, sir.' Ky nodded.

'Well, deal with it, Ky.' The Head shoved him toward the door. 'Now!'

'But-,' He turned back, stomach twisting.

'The lives of everyone in this school rest with you, Ky.'

42

┊Nightmare┊

The doze had been a mistake, even though Fay had been too tired to dream.

She'd awoken too late and missed her dinner.

Forced to forage, she only found tinga berries. Finally, she had to raid the healers' remaining bread. There was only a nub left.

The mrug had to go without too. It kept squeezing her leg, to remind her. After sharing her last berries, she just kept putting it down on the floor. There was nothing else she could do.

Still hungry, she went to look for more, but in the dark she couldn't tell what she was picking. The mrug was happy feasting on some night insects that emerged.

She'd returned to her bed as moon Barus bled over the horizon.

She expected to lie there for hours, but as soon as she closed her eyes, she plunged into nightmare.

It was dark, tinted pink. She was looking through another's eyes. Something warm pulsed in her hand, sending strange music through her head.

There was a waterfall that echoed around her, boiling into a midnight pool. Perhaps it was in a cave.

Unease filled her as a thousand crocodilian noses stippled the surface of the pool.

She looked down, recognising the

sandals she'd found for Ky. A strange, high-pitched buzz drowned the roar of falling water.

She moved closer to the pool, as if drawn there.

Staring down into the water, Ky's face looked back at her. For a moment she calmed.

The terrible face of a tmeg solidified beside his reflection, swirling mist.

'No!' Fay shrieked, thrashing helpless in her bed.

The huge head sank down, filling her vision with scale, spike and claw. Long nostrils huffed foul breath. A flicking tongue danced between enormous fangs.

She gazed hopeless into those fierce orange eyes, flicking across to Ky's wide ones.

'Ping!' Fay screamed, thrashing at the air, tangling her covers.

She woke, streaming sweat, panting.

She'd told him not to ping near a tmeg.

'Ky!'

Her hands shook. It took a few moments to kill the dark, tipping the blimworm to persuade it to light.

'Ky! Wake up!'

Shivering, she huddled under her covers, staring at the familiar walls.

Ky was gone, a dark void in her mind.

Her fingers pleated the rough fabric, in tune with the slamming of her heart.

Now she was convinced.

Something was after Ky and it looked a lot like a tmeg.

43

:Cold:

Ky pinged back out into the rain, with no idea what to do. Mum would be no help. He didn't want Dad coming after Mum just yet. Most of his other family were on Mrax.

Tate and Egan were slipping in the football-churned mud.

The stabwebber was gaining on them, its furry, column legs looking skinny in the rain, like a cat in a bath. The legs bent at crazy angles with every disco step.

Scowling, Ky thought hard.

Music had worked for him before. He fumbled out his phone. He only kept the opera track because of its previous success. Thumbing the volume to the top, he held it above his head, letting the aria ripple up through the sheeting rain.

The stabwebber didn't pause. Maybe it couldn't hear it over the water drumming on its head. It probably didn't go out in the rain on Mrax.

He changed the track to heavy rock and tried again, but still there was no response.

Tate was on his knees in a mud patch again. Egan was deserting him, legs flying.

The creature was close now.

It loomed above the pitch, its waltzing shadow reflecting in the puddle around Tate's kneeling form.

Rubbing his sore stomach, Ky glanced back. Lining the windows, the remaining pupils were watching the creature. Above them, the teachers were all looking at Ky.

Gritting his teeth, Ky pinged to Tate, yanking him up, pinging him back to the school.

'Thank me later,' he yelled, dropping him on the hall floor, pinging back outside.

Too late.

Accelerating, the creature was right behind Egan as he vanished inside. Ky could sense its fear, its cold confusion. Teachers and pupils scattered, shrieking.

It wailed as it crashed into the atrium entrance, bringing down the glass roof in a cascade of lethal shards.

Claws flailing, it ripped away more panels. Punching through walls, it forged forward, keening.

From outside, behind it, Ky watched the stream of runners disappearing out the gate.

Reluctant, he forced his feet to follow the path of destruction.

Ky saw it squeezing into the hallway, legs and claws folding in, hunching down. The dusty chandelier bounced off its head, crystal tinkling, rolling to the floor in the debris.

When it stopped rolling, Ky crept forward.

Gibbering, the creature crunched through the wall, bursting into the main hall. Here the roof was high, and it could unfold its legs, rising to its full height. Dislodged ceiling panels and lights crashed to the ground.

It stopped there, shivering, water pooling around it. It smelled of dank old socks and vinegar. The dripping silence was like a held breath.

Ky wished he had Fay's healing gifts. He couldn't know its condition, even if he could sense its intentions. Misery oozed from it.

Lingering outside the crumbling wall, he watched it.

The stabbers drooped over its face, dangling. The claws flopped on the floor. Dripping, the legs shook. It was a sorry sight.

He couldn't see any eyes, but they must be there somewhere, watching him.

Its breathing rattled. That still didn't

mean it wouldn't need a snack any minute.

Something touched his back, making Ky jump.

'What's it doing?' the Head whispered, mopping a gash on his bald head.

'Dunno. Looks to me like it's cold. It just wants to get out the rain for now.' Ky shrugged.

'Is it safe to send the students home?' the Head asked, gesturing at the broken roof and the rain turning the smashed glass, tiles and brick-dust into sludge.

'I saw a lot of them running out anyway. I reckon now is better than later. Quietly and as far from here as you can.' Ky nodded. 'It'll be hungry once it dries out.'

'You'd better stay and watch it then, Ky. You must have the right connections to get rid of it. I'll leave it to you and yours to deal with.'

Sniffing, he left, rounding up the curious who had crept back to peek.

Tugging his ear, Ky tried to think what he

could do. He'd just recovered from pinging it here. He wasn't keen to repeat that too soon.

You and yours, he'd said.

Then it came to him. His dad's brother was someone he hadn't intended telling that Mum was back. But this left him little choice.

'Uncle Dom? You around? I have a problem,' he sent, recalling the happy days he and Fay had spent at Dom's farm.

'Ky? You're back on Earth? Hey. Good to hear from you.' Dom's instant reply sent a wave of relief rushing over him.

'I need a bit of help, Unc. A stabwebber just smashed up my school.'

'Really? How d'you get a stabwebber here?'

'Long story and no idea.' He sent Dom the view from his perch.

'Are you safe?'

'Think so, for now.'

'Good. I'll be there in a minute.'

Ky allowed himself to breathe again. He found a dry patch, settling down to wait.

Rubbing his sore belly again, he wondered what had happened to Tate after he dropped him. Egan had escaped indoors just in time. They were probably the first runners out the gate.

Dripping silence descended. Everyone had gone. So now he was alone with the hitchhiker. At least it wasn't a tmeg.

Shivering, he wrung out his hair.

He could only hope the stabwebber was too cold to be hungry.

44

¦Reek¦

Dawn still spun mist from the treetops as Fay pinged to Central Eating. Ravenous, she piled her bowl from the cereal tubs until it overflowed. Splatting yoghurt on top, she carried the dripping bowl to a table where she could watch the last flares of sunrise.

For once, the fussy mrug tucked in too. She felt a pang of guilt that it had suffered because of her nap. Still, she didn't plan to repeat it.

'Ky?' She tried again, biting down on her breakfast berries. Delicious juice flooded her mouth.

There was still no response. Where was he?

'Pananas.' Fyl popped in behind her. 'Seen Ky?'

'Pananas. No. He's not answering me and I haven't seen him for a while.' Fay sighed, grimacing.

'He missed flying in the squadron this morning, but his mrug turned up.' Fyl sat beside her.

'His mrug came?' Alarm feathered up her spine. 'But he'd never leave it...'

'I know. I asked the elders. They don't know either. Balzar's in a funk because he's lost Ky's Ma, so I didn't want to worry him.'

'Ky's mum's missing too? That's too much of a coincidence. I bet I know where he's gone.'

'I suppose. He must have had a good reason. Especially if he didn't tell his pa.' Fyl frowned.

'Hmm. That's weird. Even if he took his mum home, why wouldn't he come back?' Fay chewed thoughtfully.

'He always said his mum wanted him to go back to school. Maybe he's giving in for a little while.' Fyl mused, crunching.

'Nah. He hated it.' Fay shook her head. 'Besides, he loved being in the squadron. He wouldn't want to miss it.'

'That's what I thought. He really should have been there today. Do you think someone should go find him?' Fyl flicked up an eyebrow.

'Let's give him another day. He won't stay there any longer than he has to.' Fay frowned.

If the tmeg was after him, maybe it would be a relief for him to be away from Mrax anyway.

Recalling her dream, she shuddered.

'I suppose.' Fyl gulped another mouthful.

'Why do you say he should have been there today?' Fay fed another morsel to her mrug.

'This cloud's different, huge and still growing. We found a whole dead village today, crisped where it had passed. It was eerie. Gave me the shivers. You probably treated the victims. We've reported it, anyway.'

'Mm. I've seen the cloud. It's awful.' She hugged herself, chilled by her untold dreams.

'On patrol the other day we saw all this cloud billowing up. Odd colour and it reeked. Clouds don't normally smell.' Fyl shrugged.

'They don't? Ha. I'd never really thought about it.'

'Well, we'll leave it to the Elders and Ancients. See what happens. Someone's on watch up there.' Fyl finished his bowl.

'But they'll just talk it to death! Fay slapped her hand on the table.

Fyl stared at her. 'What do you know?'

'I've seen the devastation, the injuries. We

need to do something fast.'

'All healers report please, many injured.'

They groaned together, pinging away.

45

⋮Tornado⋮

Shivering in his sopping clothes, Ky jumped when Dom pinged in beside him. His uncle scrubbed his head, with a fond hand. Ky felt better straight away.

'Good to see you Ky.' Dom peeked in. *'So the beast's holed up here.'*

'Holed is the word.' Ky looked back at the damage.

His uncle craned around the corner.

'Ha! How pathetic!' Dom shook his head.

Ky's teeth were chattering too much to grin.

'I reckon it doesn't like being wet.' Ky shrugged, feeling much the same. *'The Head said me and mine should deal with it. Then he let everyone else go home.'*

'It's definitely beyond him.' Dom nodded. *'And we don't want the government to know we brought another creature here. That would be a disaster when they're just getting used to having aliens around.'*

'But the Head will have to close the school. How can we keep it a secret?' Ky shuddered again, freezing.

'We'll have to think about that.' Dom scowled. *'Look it's as miserable as you right now. I don't think it's going anywhere. I reckon it's safe for you to pop home and I can get some advice on this. When you're all warmed up we'll sort it out. Okay?'*

'Thanks Dom.' Ky gave his arm a grateful squeeze, pinging away. *'See you soon.'*

⋮

Mum was not impressed to see Ky return from school soaked and filthy.

'School can't be closed,' she squawked. 'You've only been back a day!'

'Well, we had a bit of a problem. Sit down Mum, I'll make you some tea,' Ky replied, through chattering teeth.

'I'm quite capable of making tea, Ky!' she snapped. 'Go jump in the shower. You look frozen.'

He raced up the stairs and into the bathroom, fretting how he could explain the situation without upsetting her. He took his time, waiting until he was red as a fire squirrel and had some idea of how to start. She said she'd seen it anyway.

Emerging, rubbing his hair, he slid into his thickest winter joggers and a heavy jumper. Shoving his feet into fuzzy slippers, he crept back down the stairs.

The tea was waiting beside the pack of chocolate biscuits. She was waiting too, perched tense on a stool, the cat curled on her lap.

'You look better now.' She watched him sip.

'Thanks Mum.' He eyed her stiff pose, munching. 'You know you said you thought you saw something out in the trees...' he began carefully.

'Oh, I was just being silly after all that-'

'No you weren't, Mum! It's here. Somehow it must have hitchhiked with us when we came home. That's probably why I passed out.' He snuck another biscuit.

'What is it?' All colour drained from her face. The cat hissed. She slid to her feet, clasping it to her chest, poised to run.

'You wouldn't know it if I told you.' He shook his head, reluctant to give it a name for her imagination to fill in. 'But it's here. It smashed up the school. So I got hold of Dom. He's getting some help to deal with it.'

'Dom!' Her face lit up with relief. She sat down again. The cat gave him a dirty look and settled to her knees. 'He can send it back. So where is it now?'

'It holed up in the school hall in the dry. So we left it to-'

'You left it? You pinged back here, knowing it hitch-hiked before,' she croaked, craning out the window. 'And now no-one's watching it?'

'Dom is. I'm going right back-'

'You're not!' She snarled. The cat stood on her lap, back arched, hissing. All its long, ginger fur stood on end.

'Sorry, Mum. I have to help Dom.' He stood, setting the empty mug down. This conversation was derailing fast.

'Dit said you're a man now. She was right.' She said, bitterly. The cat moaned deep in its throat, glaring.

'We'll just send it back and everything will be fine again.' He ploughed on, feeling he'd got something wrong along the way.

'You only went back to school for me, didn't you?' Her eyes glistened.

307

The cat's fur settled down. It turned to look up at her.

'It's what you wanted. Don't cry Mum, please.' He wrung his hands, not daring to reach past the cat's claws.

'You did this on purpose, didn't you? You brought that thing-.'

'No!' He shouted over her rising tirade, shocked. 'I didn't know!'

'Go! Sort it out with your beloved uncle.' Her voice caught.

'But-,' He reached out to her. The cat swiped at his finger, baring its teeth.

'Just leave me alone!' she screeched.

Electrified, the cat leapt at him from her lap; a ginger tornado, claws out.

Dancing away, grabbing his coat, Ky left.

46

⫶Goo⫶

Fay had been healing all day. The injuries were mostly the same, burns, scalds, loss of fur, singed scales. Most of the creatures had to be hypnotised to calm them down, they were so afraid.

'I'm glad that's over.' Shaking her head, she plodded back to the healer's rest room.

'There's something not right there.' Iyam

glanced at her, lifting the door flap. Sharing a sigh, they sucked down the fragrance of fresh bread, heading for the table.

'They were sticky. They stank. That smell was on all of them.' Fay nodded, snapping the crust, grabbing a handful.

'Like Earth stink. Horrible. I don't think it was a fire at all.' Iyam wrinkled her nose, pulling a chunk from the loaf.

'Me either. I dreamed it.' Fay frowned, chomping. The mrug nibbled a crumb from her fingers.

'You did?' Mumbled Iyam, holding up her hand. 'Ahhh. I need this.'

'Me too.' Fay took another handful, biting down, savouring its nutty fragrance. 'Mmm. This smells so much better.'

'Doesn't it!' Iyam rolled her eyes, rattling the beads in her hair as she nodded. 'I'm going to talk to the rescue team. I want to know what happened. Wanna come?'

'Sure.' Grabbing another chunk for the journey, they pinged away.

⋮

The rescue team had set up camp on a rise at the edge of the plain.

'They were lying everywhere, poor things, screaming. All the ground was dark and that smell, ew.' Flyn, one of the finder team shuddered. 'They all fixed?'

'Mostly. The injuries were like burns. Did you see a fire?' Iyam touched a nearby twig, frowning at her stained fingers.

Fay gazed across the blackened landscape, not sure what to look for. How could you spot a chemical? For certain, it would not be in a phial in a lab, which was the only place she'd seen any before.

'Well, the ground's dark, scorched looking. But it wasn't a fire smell.' He shook his head. 'What else could it be?'

'Good question.' Iyam frowned, fingering one of her many braids.

'Can I help?' Another boy stepped in beside them.

'Absolutely.' Iyam smiled. Taking his arm,

311

she led him away, firing questions.

'Show me.' Fay stepped forward.

'Well, we can go this way I suppose. Mind where you walk. That sticky stuff's everywhere.' He moved forward, tucking his feet beside the shredded plants on untainted sand. Fay followed his example, holding up her mrug and her wide trouser legs.

The ground stretched away, scorched black and stinking. Bushes had been reduced to skeletons, sticky goo clotting the joints, hanging in snotty drips. Bones were all that remained of the smallest creatures, crunching underfoot. Treacly globs covered every stone, building up around the soles of her sandals.

Soon she could see the trail of fleeing footprints, a pale scar through the dark landscape.

'How far..?' He stopped, where the ground slanted away into the charred valley.

'This is fine.' Fay nodded, staring not into the distance but at the open ground around her feet. Here was the evidence she was looking for.

A thousand tiny circles pitted the surface; evidence of a lethal kind of rain. Black rain.

47

⦙Trail⦙

Ky pinged to Dom's farmhouse, steaming, to find it empty. Spreading his hands towards the huge Aga, he soaked up its warm welcome in the silence.

Mum had never acted like that before. It hurt. He couldn't decide whether to be angry.

'Dom?'

'Ky. Where are you?'

'Looking for you, at the farm.'

314

'I'm back at the school. It's still here. We're considering what to do with it.'

Ky could feel the ironic smile in his words.

'It needs to go back.' Ky nodded.

'You and I know that. It'll take them a while to come around to it.'

'What can I do?' Beside the Aga, Ky wrung his tingling hands.

'Not much, frankly. What do you want to do?'

'Well Mum threw me out, so I guess I should go back to Mrax.'

'She what?' Dom barked.

'She was upset. She saw it, just when she thought she'd left our monsters behind.'

'I see. Tricky. Well, if you want to go, I'll keep an eye on her. She'll get over it.'

'That's what I thought. Thanks. But I don't want to take it with me again.'

'Walk a long way away. That should do it.'

'That's all? Seems too simple. Thanks for sorting it out, Unc.' He was already trotting

outside.

'No problemo. Say hi to Balzar.'

'I - I will.' Ky scowled, zipping up the hill, past the power station site and the new electricity tree the Mraxi had replaced it with.

He took a deep breath, winding up his power.

'Must be far enough away now.' He puffed, stopping on a rise to look back at the village.

Focussing on Central Eating, he launched, grinning.

⋮

'Where were you?' demanded Fyl.

'You okay?' Fay stared into his eyes with a frown.

'Earth,' he whispered, shivering.

'Why did you leave your mrug?' Fyl sounded upset.

'Had to take Mum home,' he husked, with a pang. 'It hates that trip.'

'Come on. You need food.' Fay took an arm, hoisting him to his feet.

'It went back with me.' Guilt hit him like a sledge hammer. His haunted eyes scanned the surrounding trees.

'What?' Fyl hitched a brow.

'Stabwebber.' Ky shook his head, squinting into the trees.

Their stares bored into his face.

'But that's one of our-,' Fyl broke off, eyes bulging.

'How?' Fay followed his gaze into the darkling trees.

'Must have hitch-hiked.' Ky shrugged. 'Long story.'

'Food first.' Fay tugged him away.

In no time, he was squeezed at the table, scooping a delicious stew, chewing morsels of delicate fish.

Replete, he propped his head on his hands, yawning.

'So what happened? We were worried about you.' Fyl's eyes flicked to meet Fay's.

'Mum wasn't happy. So I took her home. Except that thing came too. She saw it and

317

freaked. So here I am.' Ky plastered on a wan smile.

'Not my fault. She won't believe me. I just really need to sleep.' He blinked heavy lids.

'Well you can-,'

His mrug landed over his head with a heavy plop. Ky's head slipped off his hands, slamming onto the table. Dimly he heard Fyl's guffaw.

'Oi! Gerrof.' He peeled off the jubilant mrug, rubbing his bruised chin. It turned circles around his head, red eyes gleaming, oozing delight.

'Did you miss me then?' A smile broke across his lips.

'I think it just told you that.' Fyl laughed.

'Well, I missed you too.' He reached up to snag it, scratching its nose. It wriggled onto his shoulders, overlapping on every side.

He looked back at Fay.

'I don't think I'll be able to sleep knowing the stabwebber's still there. Not that I can sleep in the cabin anyway.' Ky stretched. The mrug slid off, swooping away.

'Where do you sleep then?' Fay frowned.

'I go down to the village shelter cave.' He shrugged, feeling his ears burn.

'Whatever works, I suppose.' Fyl smiled.

'It has to go back where it came from.' Fay echoed his uncle's words. At least she wasn't glaring at him, as if he should have known all along. Dad would, when he found out.

'But-,'

'It has to be the one we met when we fell in that cave. It must have attached itself to you from there.' Fay shuddered.

'We don't know that. It was days before it turned up on Earth.' Ky tugged his ear.

'No, but it's pretty likely. They live in caves.' Fay rolled her eyes.

'Follow the time trail from the day you saw it,' Fyl suggested.

'Where did you go when you left?' Fay asked.

'Oh no.' Ky dropped his face in his hands.

319

'Mum's new house here on Mrax. I thought I saw something move in the trees.'

'Ah-ha.' Fay nodded. 'And then?'

'She was upset. I pinged her back to Earth and passed out.'

'Poor thing.' Fay grimaced. 'Not you.' She snapped at the smile in his eyes.

'Poor thing?' Ky ground his teeth.

'I didn't mean your mum either. Think about it. Maybe it didn't mean to do that. Perhaps it needed to escape the cave it had outgrown.' Fay shrugged. 'Either way, it lives in the dark, in silence. Suddenly it's travelling around Mrax in jumps and then across space. After that it's plunged into a busy world of noise and bright light. It must have been terrified.'

'Certainly terrified everyone else.' Ky pressed his lips together. 'Why does it do that weird dance, bending its legs all over?'

'It's eyes are on its knees. In a cave it can find a position for each leg so it has an all-round view.' Fyl swivelled his shoulders.

Ky blinked.

'They're webbers. They wait, mostly.' She shrugged.

'What about the stabbers?'

'Like Earth spiders, they inject their prey to liquefy the insides. The stabbers mean it can defend itself and get much bigger prey. Yum.' Fay grimaced.

'But most of the big creatures here aren't in the caves.' Ky frowned. 'How does it get big prey?'

'Excuse me a moment.' Fyl went over to talk to giggling Dav, who had Zay's head trapped under his elbow.

'Deep in the night, when Barus is up, it's open season. Everything's hunting. And where's the best sanctuary out of the moonlight?' Fay hitched a gull-wing brow.

'I'm glad I didn't think about that before.' Ky shivered recalling his feeling of sanctuary when the tmeg passed overhead.

'I reckon your dad could help you ping it, at least.' She snipped.

'That's my last resort right now.' Ky scratched his head, dreading that conversation.

'Ask. Definitely.' She nodded.

'Fay, you know stuff I don't. I need you.' Ky wrung his hands as she looked away.

'Oh! You need a pee. Here.' Fay set her mrug down, still scowling.

It floated up off the ground.

'Hey! You can fly!' Fay clapped her hands, delighted. 'Now I can walk right again!'

Ky's mrug zoomed down to greet it. They looped in the air together like fish deep underwater, oozing joy.

Fyl resumed his meal, glaring across at Dav and Zay. They ignored him, giggling.

'I think your mrug was trying to tell you something.' Ky whispered, watching the mrugs flip and roll.

'What?' Snapped Fay, staring at him.

'It can help?' Ky suggested.

'Oh Zod!' Fay dropped her head in her hands.

'Well, it's good that you're back. I have lots to tell you. But not tonight.' Yawning, Fyl stood to return his shell to the washing up pile. 'The squadron will be out as usual in the morning. Sleep well and we'll catch up tomorrow.' He vanished.

'Ugh. Sorry Fay, and thanks. I have to try to sleep too. I'm off to bed. Night.'

Waving he pinged back to the cabin.

The last thing he expected was to find it smashed to splinters once more.

He'd never sleep again.

48

⠸Bald⠸

Abandoned, Fay scowled up at the mrug, now circling her head. What help could it possibly be?

She spotted Myn and her family drinking at the waterfall. Time to go.

As she rose to slink away, the kittle squealed, bounding towards her.

She was still raising defensive hands when it leapt over the table, knocking her to the ground.

Fry, in its frilly pyjamas, planted its long legs around her. Its fat tongue licking her face, she couldn't get up.

'Fry! Bad kitty!' Myn trotted over, huffing. 'Sorry Fay. It loves you!' Her smile almost split her face.

Fay tugged it away by its ear, clambering back to her seat.

'Pananas Fry. How are you?' Grinding her teeth, Fay rubbed her sticky face on her sleeve. The kittle tried to jump on her lap.

'No you don't!' Myn pushed it down. 'If you don't want me to hold you, and you won't wear a lead, you have to behave! Hear me?' She wagged a finger, which it snapped at, wriggling.

Slowly, Myn let go. Fry dashed off to the fruit table, returning with a mingo for Fay, which it set carefully in front of her.

'How sweet! Bostril, thank you Fry.' Laughing, she stroked its bonnet.

Its long tail, in the frilly cover, quivered.

One huge, fried egg eye gazed, adoring, into her face, unless it was watching something behind, you could never tell.

'Isn't it wonderful?' gushed Myn.

'Grown any fur back yet?' Fay asked it, in the hope that her attention would calm it down. It seemed to work. Fry folded its legs, settling to the table, gazing up at her, or maybe at Myn.

Fay peeked inside the pyjamas. The blisters seemed to have healed, but the fur was still not growing. She frowned.

'I guess its skin's still getting over the trauma. I'm sure its fur will grow back soon.'

'Don't care.' Myn put out a hand. Fry ducked away. 'I love it just as it is.'

Myn's family joined them.

'C'mon Myn, it's late. Good to see you Fay. Don't stay too long.' They tugged Myn away.

Smiling, Fay watched Fry bounce after them, tail straight up. She waved, in case it was looking back at her.

Once they vanished, Fay realised she was alone. The cook fires were mere embers, glowing orange as a tmeg's eyes. A pombat flickered overhead.

She jumped from her seat, shuddering. There was too much in her head. She wouldn't sleep for hours.

She pinged away with her mrug to her favourite lookout, sitting on her usual perch. Blim soared into the sky, painting the world silver.

The mrug drifted around her, blocking out patches of stars.

After a while, the usual slinker family slid below like shadows toward their hunting grounds.

Admiring the view, cross-legged, Fay imagined it all burnt. The cloud was wrecking her world. Her toes curled.

She fretted as umbos bumped heads, shook their ears and plodded by snuffling below. Rising to follow, she stopped by the lake, staring down at her reflection.

327

Gasping, she saw that her curls had gone. Now her hair was straight on both sides of her head. She held up her hands, pearly nails glinting in the moonlight from only one.

If she was changing, it was progressing. If there was something wrong, she couldn't yet feel any effects. It felt like a stranger stared back.

Only when a hungry flitter soared overhead did she seek the warmth of her bed.

Lying under her covers, she couldn't decide which was worse, the torture of her thoughts or the terror of her nightmares.

In the end she had no choice.

49

⋮Tongue⋮

Shouting jerked Ky from his exhausted slumber. Dragging up his eyelids he could see only darkness. He frowned, yawning.

Fumbling out his phone, he flicked on the torch.

Squinting as the cave reared into view, memory flooded back. The cabin. Even here in the cave, it was hours before he'd calmed enough to sleep.

⋮

Stretching, he knuckled his eyes.

Voices drifted in. The squadron! Scratching, he jumped into his clothes, pinging up to the green beside the cabin.

Flyers were squawking. The voices were suddenly much louder, coming closer.

From the trees, he saw the squadron hovering, where the cabin had again become a heap of splinters. Jax and Dit's works of art were again smashed or scattered. He sighed.

With a pang he realised he hadn't even looked for his chest yet. Last night was just a blur of terror.

'There you are!' yelled Fyl, waving. 'I can't believe it happened again.'

Ky clambered over the splinter pile, earning a few scratches on the way.

His mrug slapped down over his head.

'Good morning, to you too.' He smiled, peeling it off.

'Want some help here?' Fyl suggested.

'Thanks. Can someone just cruise about

and see if you can spot the tmeg?' Ky scratched his head, stretching, as one mrug floated away.

'A tmeg did thith?' Tytus stared at him.

'Happens a lot.' Ky nodded, rubbing gritty eyes.

'Too much,' put in Fyl gazing down, grim.

'Can anyone see my chest?' Ky croaked, trotting to drink water from the stream. It was icy with the dawn.

'I found it!' Byran yelled. 'It's all scratched up but it's still locked.'

'The tmeg?' Ky stiffened, quaking inside.

'No tmeg's about,' Snyz hollered, circling high on the tip of one mrug wing, whooping. They made a diamond silhouette against the sunrise.

'Good.' Rubbing his arms, Ky summoned his mrug. 'Well, there's not much I can do about the cabin now.' He clambered on board, the mrug rolling its eyes. 'We can fix it up later.'

'S'pose not.' Fyl stared down at the mess.

'Let's go then.' They floated up.

The squadron reformed around him. The ground dropped away.

'You said you had a lot to tell me?' Ky hitched an eyebrow.

'Better still, we'll show you.' Beckoning, Fyl, swooped up towards the sun.

⋮

The brownish cloud hung over the canyon, dark, rank and ominous. Staring, Ky squeezed the tendrils in his fists. The mrug's eyes flicked up at him, then back.

'It's bigger.' He shivered, suddenly cold.

'Come a bit closer, so you can smell it.' Fyl floated towards it, the squadron ranged around them.

'It stinks!' Byran held his nose through the scarf.

'I know.' Ky wrinkled his nose. The acrid stench burnt his nostrils. 'Is it the same underneath?'

'Hadn't thought of that. Let's take a look.'

Fyl tipped down, away from the stench.

'What do the Ancients say?' Ky followed, hanging on against the g-force. 'Ugh.' He spat out a bug.

'Nothing yet. Fay thinks they're taking too long. We're waiting.' Fyl hovered at the lip of the canyon. 'I wonder if it's connected to the draining of the sour sea? Bet that went when we had the earthquake and the eclipse together. It's only over there.' He waved an arm.

Foul fog boiled in front of him, taller and spreading in beige and lilac billows further along the canyon.

'There's no way down without going into it.' Snyz peered along the cliff.

'What about from the end?' Ky frowned.

'It'th a dead end that way.' Tytus pointed left. 'But there might be an open end that way.'

'Let's try.' Fyl wheeled to the right. 'Keep a close watch. Don't want the wind to change and blow it over us.'

They cruised along the cliff edge for a long time. The cloud towered higher, spilling over the edges towards them.

'It's huge.' Ky scratched his head. 'The sun isn't burning it off.'

'That's what we told the Ancients. Personally, I don't think they have a clue what it is or what to do about it.'

⋮

Ky's legs were cramping by the time they reached the end of the fog-filled canyon.

Between the cliffs, the cloud shrank into the space until just a wedge hung out like a ghostly tongue licking the beach.

White-capped waves dashed at the crumbling rocks where the cliffs sank down to the beach. Sea flyers mewed, hanging on the wind.

The mrugs settled to the shingle, obviously relieved for a break too. Freed of their passengers, they were soon splashing in their element.

'Let's take a closer look.' Tytus turned, plodding towards the fog tongue.

Following, the stench soon had them all coughing.

Ky hopped up on a boulder, staring into the gloom beneath it.

'Look,' he croaked, pointing into the clear space in the bottom of the canyon.

The others joined him frowning, choking.

'The plants are all dead,' Byran quavered.

'Thith ith theriouth,' Tytus moaned.

'Everything's black in there, like it's burnt,' whispered Snyz.

'It's a killer cloud.' Fyl nodded.

As they watched, the misty tongue extended slowly towards them. They were plunged into shadow.

'Time to go.' Ky hopped down, loping away. The others followed, eager to leave.

Suddenly, he felt it again; the tingle. That high pitched buzz in his ears. Oh no. His eyes scanned for those familiar spikes.

Shuddering he faced the sea, watching

each wave hump up, to crash foaming on the shore.

'Ky! Have you seen your mother?' Dad's stern voice rang through his head. He jumped.

Wincing, Ky watched the boys mount up at the shoreline as the buzzing grew. His father would be livid. How often had he called Dad with no reply? Good. Let him stew.

He'd left Mum there alone, knowing the stabwebber was still there. He chewed his cheek, torn. Maybe it came back to Mrax with him.

The last thing he wanted was to go back.

If he stayed there was no escape. If he went to Earth, Dad was a long way away. So were the tmeg and the eels.

Mum needed him. He'd been looking after her ever since Dad left them years ago. He couldn't stop now. His chin wobbled.

The boys beckoned, floating up on the wind. Would they call him chicken if they knew?

'I can't, guys. Sorry. There's something I have to do. See you later.' He waved them away.

'You won't want to come with me.' Standing by the mrug, smoothing its tendril, he sent it a picture of the crushed cabin. It wasn't as though he had a home left, either. It was just somewhere the mrug could wait for him.

The huge red eyes glared back at him as he wound up his power.

Slowly, broadcasting distress, the mrug trailed after the others, eyes flicking back to watch.

'You okay?' Yelled Fyl, circling.

'I need to go. Now.' His stomach churned.

Ky pinged, praying he was space-jumping alone.

50

⁝Melting⁝

Fay crept from her wrecked bed, hooking up her blimworm. The night had been long and hard. She could not greet the morning with any enthusiasm.

'Ky?'

Silence echoed hollow where Ky should have been. Fay frowned, climbing to her feet.

'All healers report tonay, please, mass injuries.' Groaning, she tugged on her clothes,

emerging into the throng rushing down the corridor.

'What happened?' she asked, elbowing in, the mrug floating above her.

'The cloud moved,' someone answered from behind.

'Scores of injuries,' put in another voice.

Fay was swept into the main cavern. There were no squeals or roars, no cries of pain. She stopped. The crowd milled, confused.

One corner of the room lit up green. The crowd settled, waiting for the Ancients to speak.

'Healers, there are many cases awaiting your talented hands. However, we wish to take a moment to keep you all up to date, so you know what we face.'

Murmurs rustled through the crowd. The Ancients waited for silence.

'By now, you will know that there is a strange cloud moving over the continent causing much suffering. We have been

scouring the Legends for any similar references. Last night, we found mention of it in one of the oldest archives.'

Expectant silence filled the cavern.

'Sadly the Legend describes scores of losses and injuries but not how or indeed if, the cloud was overcome.'

Muttering broke out. The Ancients again waited for silence.

'So we are in the rare situation where there is no guidance. Anyone who has any success, either in healing or in combating the effects, is to report it. We will listen to all and any suggestions or thoughts. The good news is that we are still here, so we must have prevailed before.'

Fay straightened her back. The mrug dropped over her head, blinding her. She fought it off, spinning it away, tutting.

'So we will leave you to tend the many new victims of the cloud. Your proud devotion to your calling may save us all. Please share any breakthroughs. We need

every advantage to beat this menace. Working together, we will prevail.' The Ancients' green presence faded.

Teams began to assemble as new patients arrived. Two kittles, burned bald and wailing arrived first. They gave off a familiar acrid stench. The sound made her blood run cold.

A flitter arrived, all claws and wings, keening. Its scales were damaged, its wings full of holes and melting.

A man staggered in, gritting his teeth against the pain, his hair burned away.

Ignoring her mrug's reproachful eyes, Fay rolled up her sleeves, steeling herself against the screams of pain.

Digging in, she struggled to concentrate knowing Ky had disappeared again.

51

⁞Storm⁞

It was a freezing night on Earth, the wind buffeting Ky almost off his feet as he appeared at the back door. Setting his ear to the wet glass, he could hear the TV blaring.

'Mum!' Peering between the curtains he could see his mother side-on, sipping from a cup. He tapped on the door. Visions of the warm parka waiting in his bedroom, crowded in.

Immediately a fluffy ginger head rose from her lap, hissing. Ky hesitated, then tapped again, louder.

She didn't move, probably couldn't hear him over the din. Maybe she didn't want him there.

Stinging sleet slapped at him, rattling on the glass. The cat's eyes gleamed.

'Mum!' He yelled, rapping again, hopeless.

Still she stared glassy-eyed to the side. The cat's defiant, emerald glare didn't waver.

Perhaps she still didn't want to see him. Her last words rolled through his head.

Sighing, soaked, he pinged back to the school. The weather felt like punishment.

The damaged roof had slid further, rocking now, groaning in the wind. Painful, sideways hail was turning the wreckage into a swamp.

'Dom?' Shivering, he tiptoed between brick and metal, crunching on grit and glass. *'I'm back.'* The spars of the atrium groaned above, showering splinters, shaking cables.

343

He ducked into the shattered corridor, following the path of destruction into the dark. The only light came from a single, blinking emergency light. Snaking wires, sparked like tiny, lethal fireworks.

Which would be worse, if it had pinged back with him already, or if it waited here for him in the dark?

The main hall wall was a heap of crumbs. He peered toward the back of the room, dark as a mine. The floor seemed to be moving. He peered down, but couldn't tell. Was it there? Hesitating, Ky bit his lip.

He took a pace forward, intrigued by the swirling on the floor. As he watched it around his feet, the shadow crept up his leg.

'Ky! It's out!' Dom's voice in his head made him jump.

He dashed outside into the bouncing hail. Thunder clapped loud as he cleared the atrium. A landslide of glass and metal crashed to the ground behind his leaping feet.

In a flick of lightning, through nets of ice lace, he saw the stabwebber staggering across the field, skipping back over the goals. Fay's words came back to him. She was right. The creature was probably terrified. He wasn't happy out in the storm either.

He took off against the wind, balls of ice bouncing off him like fleas. The churned, ice piled field tripped him. Numb, spitting mud and grass, he leapt up, chasing after the dancing creature.

It scuttled across field after field, fast. He couldn't keep up, pinged closer time and again. Suddenly it stopped. He materialised almost under its feet, freezing.

Lightning strobed, flashing the creature's jagged dance in weird slow-motion. Breathless, behind it, he could see the distinctive outline of Stonehenge.

The creature gibbered, excited. It scrambled over the stones, danced around them, demented. Another flash set it leaping in fright, knocking the standing stones to the

345

ground like dominoes. The echoes of impact trembled under his feet.

'Oh, no!' There was nothing he could do right now. Somehow they would have to restore the monument before morning.

The beast staggered off, past another electricity tree that sparked in the rain. Now all he could do was keep up.

Pinging forward three more times, he emerged into the sleeping town. Its weird, leggy shadow drifted across the shopfronts around the market square.

There were silhouettes here too, figures running like him, Dom and the others. They blinked on and off, his uncle tall and broader than the rest. Relief glowed inside him.

'I see you Dom!' He sent, slipping again in a puddle. *'Ow!'*

'I see you! Why didn't you ping?'

'I was. Saw you and forgot.' Ky slid to a halt, feeling stupid. He could have pinged into his bedroom too. Now he couldn't feel his legs or arms. If he chewed his lip off, he

wouldn't know.

'We're trying to chase it toward the woods and failing. Oh no! Not the cathedral!' Dom cut off.

Squinting, Ky saw the creature change direction, aiming for the familiar solidity of ancient stone. Gibbering, it smashed the arching doors with its claws, vanishing inside.

'No!' Ky groaned as precious glass sprayed outward. The doorway collapsed in an avalanche of dust and hand-carved stone. He sprinted forward again.

Dull thuds, ominous dongs and screeches rang out through the crumbling hole. Columns groaned and crashed like felled trees, splintering pews. The famous spire leaned slowly to one side with a dull crunch. Something fluttered up there, squawking, invisible in the dark. Debris pattered and plonked to the grass beneath.

Slogging fast through the deluge, he ducked as thunder crashed overhead.

Lightning flashed. Ky winced as the topmost cross swung down with a screech.

He hunkered against the walls with the others. The team's ring of grim faces lit up clear in another flash like gargoyles. Ky tugged his numb ear.

The vicious wind howled, driving hail like bullets. He clung to a corner, yearning to get away from the howling storm. But not inside with that monster.

'It has to go back.' Dom's voice rang in his head. Everyone nodded, looking at Ky.

'I need some help.' Gulping, Ky jutted his chin. *'The cathedral's wrecked and we need to put Stone Henge back together too.'*

'One thing at a time. Show us where it came from.' Dom urged, as the others nodded.

Gritting his clacking teeth, Ky showed them where they'd emerged from the stabwebber's cave. As the team's heads nodded agreement, he felt the crackle and chill as their combined power merged and grew.

He tried to hold back, so he had some strength for later. Failed. He could feel the power sucking out of him into the maelstrom. His teeth ached.

'We have to get closer.' Ky peeked at the abominable ice wave that rushed between the stones. *'Now!'*

Ky dashed to the broken entrance, hesitating as slates smashed down from the creaking tower above. Power whirled, crackling within him, worse than any storm.

He couldn't see the creature, but that didn't mean it wasn't right there in the dark, waiting to pounce. Shivering, he scraped ice from his lashes.

The team piled behind him, pushing him forward. Furious power swirled around them, merging, swelling, alive.

In a dubious cluster, they shuffled through the rubble out of the storm. Bells chimed inside, setting off a panicked shriek in the dark.

Peering in, another bolt of lightning showed the stabwebber clambering up enormous organ pipes set both sides of the aisle.

A blast of wind through the broken doorway gave the pipes an eerie hum.

It hung there, straddling the gap, dark against the flash-lit vaulted ceilings. Claws snipping the air, it keened.

Under its weight, a fat section of pipes peeled back from the wall with a crack. It gibbered in terror, scattering dust.

'What is that dust falling off it?' Ky scratched his leg, frowning.

'Mites. They keep it clean.' Dom crept closer.

'But they're everywhere! How do we kill them?' Ky tugged his ear, watching the mite-shadow spread into gloom.

'Kill?' Dom glared at him.

The creature fell to the floor, with a clatter of metal on stone.

The organ pipes sighed a long, slow

chord as another gust whooshed in. A snowstorm of songsheets took off into the air.

Wedged in the aisle it scrabbled to escape, keening. The clawing, hissing, scratching rang loud.

Managing to right itself, it sidled away, legs up one wall, clambering over a carved wooden partition.

Another flash of lightning lit its bulk as one claw slipped out of sight.

Ky jumped as a deep organ blast filled the space, bouncing off the walls. The creature convulsed, shooting out sticky threads, stabbing at the pews, dancing demented.

'It looks like all its legs are moving in the wrong directions!' Ky snorted. 'Ha!' His laugh rang out loud in the sudden silence.

Horrified, he slapped his hands over his mouth.

A shiny crisp bag blew in the door. The mites engulfed it.

The creature froze, trembling. The stench of cheesy old socks billowed. The crisp bag vanished.

'It's seen us.' The voice in his head accused.

Swirling power crackled between them.

'Let's go quick.' Ky urged, unprepared for the sudden, howling blast of space.

52

¦Stink¦

In the healer's rest room, there was an air of celebration as they filled up with dark bread and mingo juice. The onslaught was over.

'I can't wash that stink from my hands,' Eryl moaned, scrubbing again at the tap, her rainbow scalp shining.

'I thought they'd never stop coming!' Iyam exclaimed, munching.

'We need to find out what this is made

of.' Fay sniffed her fingers, grimacing. 'The Ancients aren't doing anything.'

'It's like acid. It melts right through the fur to the skin. Even that flitter's scales were seared, and they're pretty tough.'

'It goes straight through the wings.' Fay shivered.

'I know.' The beads in her hair rattled as Iyam nodded.

'I have to be somewhere.' Fay pocketed another handful of the loaf 'See you later.'

She took off, before anyone could say another word.

'Ky?'

There was still no reply.

In her room, she washed again. Hopping into a change of clothes, she headed out, flipping her hair back over each shoulder.

She pinged to Ky's cabin, only to find it swarming with carpenters, being rebuilt again. There was no sign of Ky.

The carpenters hadn't seen him.

Yet, greeting her mrug was his, swooping

down from the heights.

She plopped onto a stump as realisation hit her.

There were only two possibilities. The tmeg had caught him during the last attack or he'd returned to Earth.

She stared up at his mrug as the two drew circles in the sky. It would know if the tmeg caught him.

Connecting she could not detect any distress, so he must be safe, so far as the mrug could tell. Which didn't mean much if Ky was on Earth.

Checking through her own mrug, it sensed a little tension.

His poor friend must be missing him.

Ky must have gone back to Earth as they suspected. She knew how bad that had been for him.

It was something he dreaded.

He must have had no choice.

53

⋮Crust⋮

Ky sprawled in a blue bush, shivering. Blinking ice off his lashes, he watched the stabwebber smack onto the ground, legs flopping.

A startled ugawuga honked, lumbering off into the rainbow trees gilded with sunrise. The clearing filled with the twitter and cheep of flyers.

Maybe the stabwebber was dead. Slowly,

he raised his head to take a better look.

'Dom? It's back home,' he tried, but his call fell into a void. So far, the only one he could talk to across space was his dad. Now he was back on Mrax, he'd have to talk to him soon. Groaning, he wriggled his cold shoulders, leaning up to peep at it again.

Ice crusted the fur on its long, folded legs. The smooth biker-helmet dome where the head should be, glistened with frost.

Craning higher he could see its armoured belly rimed in lines like ribs. Squinting he made out the faceted, fly eyes on its knees. Every spike he could see had a tip of ice, except for the tips of the stabbers which leaked black poison.

Slowly he pulled himself to his feet. His clothes cracked as he moved. He ached with it too, frozen to the core.

Delving deep, he found a crumb of power, risking more cold to spin it up.

He stared at the multitude of furry legs, folded up every which way, like a broken umbrella. On bony arms the serrated claws dangled open, not quite so scary right now. The stabbers stretched out like a display of giant spears.

As he watched, a chunk of ice slid from one sharp elbow joint, down to a claw.

As it dropped, the claw twitched. Perhaps it was just the weight of the water.

He shivered.

Willing his trembling legs to carry him, he backed into the trees. He was still waiting for that fainting feeling to wash over him. Maybe he had enough help.

Right now, he'd give anything for a hot bath and warm, dry clothes.

He dare not ping away if it meant he'd take it with him.

'Fay? I'm back.' He sent her the location view with a sudden burst of hope.

There was no answer. She must be working.

He took another peek.

The webber hadn't moved, but as he

watched, that claw twitched again. There was no ice left to explain it this time.

He shivered, waiting. It didn't move again.

He sighed, trying Fay again. She was still busy.

He scratched his knee, suddenly noticing a tickle. Looking down he saw a dark shadow moving on his leg. Peering closer, he saw the mites had survived a drenching and space travel.

'Awesome,' he whispered.

He craned for another peek at the stabwebber. Had that eye been set that way before? He backed further away, brushing the mites off his leg.

Out of sight behind a huge tree, Ky jogged on the spot. Plugging into his phone, he found some favourite tracks and danced. As the sun rose up the sky, he spun, shuffled, hopped. His clothes began to steam.

At last, he was finally feeling human again, even if his stomach kept twisting.

He took another peek from behind the

359

tree. The view turned him icy cold all over again.

The claws were flailing. The legs flexed, giving it all-round vision once more.

Ky ducked back, feeling his pulse race. If it came for him now, there was no escape.

'Fay! I need you now!' he sent, loud with panic.

'Okay! No need to shout. Where are you?'

Ky sagged with relief. He sent her an image of his view.

'Bring me food and clothes, quick. The stabwebber's on the move.'

'You're not going to pass out again, are you?' She sounded concerned.

'No. I'm fine now I've warmed up. I had some help bringing it back.' He smiled.

'I'll be there soon.' Fay was gone.

Cautious, Ky peered around the tree again.

Its fly eyes were swivelling on its knees. He ducked back, heart thumping.

At a scraping sound, he peeped again.

It began to organise its legs, one by one. The claws snipped at the trees. The stabbers rose with ominous threat.

Slowly, it rose up to its full height.

54

┆Sparks┆

Fay's feet thumped down on the familiar, crumbled hill where they had last emerged from the cave.

The giant stabwebber, stood shivering on the path. Too close. All its knees shuffled around to focus its fly eyes on her. She began to back away as the mrug circled above it.

'Ky?'

'Fay! Ooh you brought my stuff. Look left,

two big trees back.'

She caught Ky's peeking eye and nodded, still stepping backward. Quick eyes taking in her changed appearance, he laid a finger over his lips.

The stabwebber hadn't moved. All its intent eyes were focused on her. It stank of vinegar.

'If I ping, I'll take it with me. Same could apply to you. Run toward those rocks and I'll meet you there.' Ky pointed.

Fay took off. The anxious mrug soared above her.

At her sudden movement the creature leapt forward. The stabbers snapped down. She dodged. Sparks flew up off the rocks. Gasping, she ducked. Its claws scythed over her head. She leapt on a sapling. It flicked back up behind her. The stabwebber hissed, confused.

Panting, Fay crouched behind a rock feeling just like a human.

Suddenly, she connected with the mrug,

gaining a flyers' eye view from above. The world swam as the giant bug stopped, shuffling its feet.

'So it went to Earth?' She forced herself to concentrate.

The stabwebber danced away. Fay yanked herself from the mrug's consciousness.

'Yup. Smashed up the school.' Ky grinned at her, taking the clothes off her shoulder with trembling hands. *'Thanks. I'll just pop over here.'* He sidled behind a bush.

'So you brought it back. And the mites.' Fay watched his thrown clothes hit the ground with a soggy slap.

'Ahh. That's better.' He emerged, shrugging into the woolly waistcoat, hooking the clothes over bushes to dry. *'It's where it belongs. Not sure about the mites it left behind though.'*

'The mites are great. They won't hurt Earth. Here I brought food.' She fished the loaves out of her pockets.

'Yum!' Ky snatched the first, filling his mouth. The disappearing bag floated back into his mind. He smiled. *'The mites ate a plastic crisp bag. They could make a big difference on Earth.'*

'They eat anything.' Fay nodded, grinning back. *'And they breed like mad.'*

Ky scanned around the tree.

'Uh-oh. It's gone.' He frowned, dashing up the path. Chomping, he ducked as they reached the brow of the hill.

Together, they craned their necks, peeking over bushes.

'Where is it?' Fay peered down the empty slope, biting her lip.

'On the loose.' Ky groaned.

55

⋮Ripe⋮

'I need to show you something.' Ky gathered his soggy clothes, thinking she looked strange.

'That sounds mysterious.' Fay hitched an eyebrow, smoothing her long hair.

'I'm sick of worrying what to do. You're the best person to help me.' Ky licked his lips. 'Possibly the only one.'

Keeping that golden secret so long

seemed stupid now.

'I'm worrying what to do about the cloud. The Ancient's don't seem to be doing anything. They've asked us to help. It's causing so much pain and damage...' She closed her eyes.

'What have they tried?' Ky reached for her hand, towing her along the path. 'We just need to get a safe distance away to ping.'

'They looked up Legends.' Fay shrugged, jogging to keep up.

'Seriously? Don't you have experts on geology or something?'

'All sorts. They always discuss, discuss. You know.' She rolled her eyes.

'Just like Earth.' Laughing, Ky pinged them away.

⋮

'The carpenters have rebuilt the cabin already!' Fay smiled, sniffing fresh wood.

'It happened again.' Ky began to shake. For a while he'd been able to forget. 'Wow. Someone even made the bed and put my chest in.' He yanked his ear.

'I expect the squadron pitched in.' Fay stepped inside, pursing her lips.

Tugging out the chest, he wondered which wise words were trapped there.

'This is even more important, now.' Retrieving the key from its hiding place, he ground it in the lock.

'What dark secrets do you hide in there?' Fay dropped to her knees beside him, yelping as she knelt on her hair.

The lid sprang up. That delicate music drifted into his head, a fairy harp.

'I feel a song...' Neck released, Fay tipped her head, listening.

Rummaging to the bottom, he tugged out the old waistcoat. Sliding his fingers into the pocket, he found what he sought.

He twirled it aloft. It shone liquid gold in the sun. Those delicate traceries still shifted on its surface like something alive.

'I think this is the problem.' Ky laid it over his hand. 'I took it from the vine that hung over the waterfall in the cave. I thought it might be a seed pod for those flowers.'

'It's beautiful.' Fay stroked it, watching the patterns respond to her finger. 'Wish I'd seen them.'

'That's what I thought.' Ky nodded, frowning at her blue nails, keeping one eye on the mrug outside as it chased down a flyer.

'So this is your secret.' Her eyes glowed, mesmerised as she stared at the pod.

'My cabin's been wrecked twice, and Fyl's barn. By a tmeg. And I think those eels from the cave are tracking me down too.'

'Weird.' She frowned, still gazing spellbound at the pod.

'Like your nails. I thought you'd know what to do.' Ky gazed at her, fighting the magnetism of the pod.

'Me? Ha. This is way beyond me.' She was staring at it, eyes fixed. So was he.

Shaking his head to clear it, he zipped the seed into his pocket. Music seemed to sing through his leg, but his head felt clearer. Fay blinked, shaking her bows.

'I, I wondered about the Listeners.' He scratched his chin.

'Hmmm.' Fay stood, tossing her head, fingering the clip on her tunic. Her mrug hovered above her head.

'I'm gonna call the folks together again. They helped me when I lost you.' Ky closed his eyes, her outraged stare burning through his eyelids.

⋮

The Ancients' comforting green lights filled the cabin. At the front of the crowd, Grandad Jax and Grandma Dit wrapped him in their delicate arms.

Wrestling out of their tangling, soft clothing he stepped back for Fay, who hugged them too. She seemed more used to them than he. Dit giggled, delighted.

'Bananas everyone. I'm sorry to bother you but I need your advice. Firstly, I found this.' Ky laid the pod on his hand.

Gasping, Dit immediately pinched her nose, stepping back.

'Don't breathe. Quick! Pinch or it'll get to you.'

His mrug floated down from the roof to look, Fay's hovering close by.

'You know what it is?' Frowning, he took it closer to the green glow, batting away the nosy mrug.

'*Unfortunately, yes. That is a pod from the Chime vine.*' Tryn, Balzar's grandfather, told him.

'*So why do we hear music from it?*' Ky felt a twinge of dismay at his tone.

'*It means you have trespassed in the holy cavern.*' Tryn snapped, in his head. Disapproval rang loud, prickling Ky's skin.

Fay's mrug drifted through the green light, cruising circles.

'*Fay and I were chased into the caves by a tmeg.*' Ky flipped his hands out.

'*Ah. A Listener,*' Great-grandad Dex put in, his green light shimmering.

371

'We were split up, lost. I came into a cavern with a waterfall and this beautiful vine.' Ky bristled.

'The Sanctum,' Tryn intoned, reverent, several other voices joining him in Ky's head.

'Maybe the tmeg drove us there for a reason.' Fay stepped to his side.

'It knew.' Dex's voice sounded certain.

Their droning stopped immediately. Ky could feel them thinking. The pale mrug flitted back up to join his beneath the rafters.

'You attacked the Chime, stole its children.' One clipped voice bit back: Boyng, barely visible at the back.

'No, no, no! It was like it called me. I just-' Ky shook his head, tugging his ear hard.

'He didn't know! The scent probably affected him. He's still learning, remember!' Dit joined their defence, setting a frail arm across each of their shoulders.

'Blood of mrugs! This is one of the first things he should know. Balzar should have taught him better,' Boyng snapped.

372

Stomach churning, Ky wondered if Dad had found Mum yet. Would he ever be forgiven?

'Take that up with Balzar, not Ky.' Dit squeezed his shoulder.

Ky opened his mouth to protest, but he was cut off.

'We would have expected better of Fay, at least,' another voice piped up.

Ky ground his teeth at the look of shame on her face.

'I'm beginning to see what Dad was trying to save me from.' Ky glowered. *'I came to you for help.'*

Again, in the silence, he could feel the fizz of them thinking.

'We will consider the tmeg's part in this. And yours,' Tryn's voice echoed through his head.

'While you think,' Ky sniped back. *'I need you to tell me what to do about the eels and the tmeg that keep wrecking my grandparents' cabin. I suppose they were*

373

hunting for this.' He dangled the golden seed, awed again by the flickering patterns that swirled on it. 'Sorry Dit, Jax, I'll fix it again...'

Nodding, Dit pinched her nose harder.

'Indeed. The eels are the Listeners of the sacred stream. The Listener tmeg will also be hunting for it.'

'What if I put it back?' Ky bit his lip.

'It was torn from the vine. It will not grow.' Dex put in.

'I didn't tear-'

'Too dangerous! Dit snapped.

'What if it's ripe, ready to grow from the new seeds? Maybe that's why it called him,' Fay broke in, taking his hand. He felt a spark jump between them.

In the buzzing silence, Ky stared at the golden pod, strangely detached from his anger. He could somehow see inside; new life ready to burst out. Fay pulled her hand away.

He was suddenly back on his feet, a wave of realisation bursting over him.

'Cool.' He grinned at her. *'She's right. It*

must have needed a way to take the seeds away, to find somewhere new to grow.'

Ky strained to understand the hum of the Ancient's conversation. Sparks flew amid the lime glow.

Fay's mrug drifted through the green glow again, rolling those big scarlet eyes. His swooped close, concerned at the atmosphere.

'What's happening?' Ky turned to Fay.

'I dink you should dake dis bobent to disabbear,' Dit suggested, pushing them, nose still pinched. 'Your Pa's looking for you, Ky.'

'But we haven't asked about the stabwebber yet!' Ky remembered, conveniently.

'That looks like a big argument to me.' Fay grinned, then frowned. 'That scent's making me feel a bit weird.' She rubbed her temple.

'Pinch your doze.' Dit advised, pushing her forward. 'Maybe you bedder go home.'

'Come on.' Turning, Jax led the way outside.

'What about the pod?' Hesitating, Ky found the idea of putting it down suddenly difficult.

'Let dem deal wid it, when dey've finished arguing. Leave it.' Dit followed Jax outside.

Ky stared into the pod's golden depths, reaching out to set it on the floor by the Ancients. Somehow, it clung. His fingers wouldn't release it. He shook his hand. It stuck like glue.

'Dit! I can't-' He tried again. Shook it, scraped it off. It just slapped back on his palm with a mind of its own.

After four more attempts, he gave up.

'I can't put it down,' he told Jax and Dit, outside. 'What can I do?'

'If you were dat plant, where would you want your babies to live?' Fay frowned above her pinching fingers. She swayed.

Ky caught her as she began to crumple. With a wave Fay shook off his hand and took their advice, pinging away.

'I doe just de blace!' Grinning, Dit took their hands, pinging them away together.

56

⫶Tough⫶

Away from the influence of the pod, Fay soon felt better. Still concerned, she invited her Pa to come for a walk. To her great surprise, he appeared moments later.

They ambled off into the trees, Fay clenching her fists in her pockets.

Wild kittles called from leafy cover, setting off a chorus of grumpy flyers. Fay's footsteps crunched on twigs blown down in yesterday's storm. The scent of crushed herbs teased her nostrils. She barely noticed a fire squirrel running across the path just ahead, scattering fallen leaves. Her mrug noticed though, chasing it away.

'What do you know about stabwebbers?' she began, hopefully, avoiding his stare.

'I've dissected a few, mostly small ones. Tough, fur covered exoskeleton. Hard to catch the big ones. They're clever and pretty fierce.'

'There's one that's attached itself to Ky. He's been pinging it around without realising.' She watched Pa's eyebrows jump.

'I've known a tmeg do that, but not a stabwebber.' Voyn shook his head.

'It's huge. Probably ancient,' Fay offered.

'Well, I think it's unlikely it developed any skill. Maybe Ky's skill to ping is not focused enough. Maybe he's scraping up things around him, unaware. What happened to it?'

'I believe he pinged it to Earth when he took his Mum back, unless someone else did.'

'Oh no! We don't need another reason for the humans to fear us.' Voyn scowled.

'Oh, it's okay, he brought it back. But he said it smashed up the school, Stonehenge and the cathedral.'

'Oh dear. I'll put the word out, see if we can fix it all up. Was it long ago?' Grim, he nodded.

'A day or two I think.' Fay frowned. Maybe she was confusing the days. 'Thanks.'

She kicked an innocent bush, sending up a host of spinners on their helicopter wings.

'Balzar can give Ky some focussing exercises anyway, won't hurt.'

'Great. Ky hardly sees his Pa lately.' Fay twisted her fingers.

'I thought that's why he came?' Voyn frowned. 'Or was it so he could come of age?'

'I don't think he knows about that yet. He's already taken his place as a man here, hasn't he?'

'Well, he hasn't done the Challenges has

he?' Voyn's eyebrows leapt under his fringe.

'I don't think so. Although, wouldn't some of things he has done count?'

'They're not the prescribed Challenges are they? But that applies to you too, I suppose. You have both um, contributed. Hmm. I'll talk to the committee.' Voyn rubbed his chin.

The wind roared through the tree tops far overhead. The stream beside them took on a pewter sheen. She could smell the oncoming rain on the tainted gusts.

Maybe the storm wasn't finished with them yet.

'Something bad's coming, Pa. I don't think we can stop it. I'm afraid.' She rubbed her arms.

'Well I told you about the earthquakes and the mudslides. The good news is the eclipses are almost done. Still, I'm sure you're worrying about that cloud.' He grunted, nodding. 'We're doing what we can.'

For a moment, she had to blink hard.

'Talking, yeah. That's what the Ancients do. Pa, it rains death! I dreamed-' She blurted.

'Ah-ah.' Frowning, Pa wagged a finger.

'But we need-'

'Stop it Fay! Whatever I say will not change fate. Nor will it help you, as you well know.' He smiled into her eyes. 'You need some time to think. You healers are too much in demand. Take a break.'

Fay could only glare at him, feeling the blood pound through her veins.

'I will when you do.' She clenched her jaw.

'I like your hair, by the way.' He reached out to smooth it. 'What did you do?'

'Nothing Pa. One side went first, then the other, and my nails, look...' She held out her hands, gasping. 'Both hands now.'

'I like the colour.' He stared into her eyes. 'You're the healer.'

'I don't feel anything wrong.' Fay shrugged tucking her fists away.

'Like I said, maybe you need a break.' Voyn scratched his head.

'Maybe when this is all sorted out. I hope you have some plans.'

Pa laughed, shaking his head. 'I have a few ideas. I just need the Ancients to-'

'All healers report tonay.'

Cringing as the call clanged through her head, she threw up her arms.

'See? No hope. What now?' Pinging away, she waved, rolling her eyes.

Had the future she'd seen coming, arrived?

57

¦Breathe¦

'This is a waste of time. We've almost been blown off the Golden Tower and frozen at the top of Panchak. We nearly drowned when the tide rushed into the Cliff Sea Palace. And I'm still sore where the hot spring tried to poach us under the sacred arch.' Five pings later, Jax folded his damp arms, glowering. 'That slither-pit almost finished us in the flying garden. And now we're in the middle of a skinny arch spanning two cliffs. Far too high. I don't want to find out what's up here. So much for your great ideas.'

'I doan understand! Dey were such good ideas! Why won't dey let you put dem down?' Dit was scratching her head.

'Maybe I have to hold them until they're ready?' Ky shrugged. 'Why are you still pinching your nose?'

'Doan want de scent to get to be.' Dit raised a slanted eyebrow.

'There is no scent!' Jax rolled bloodshot eyes.

'You doe how suscetible I ab!' Dit exclaimed, stamping her foot.

Playful, the mrug circled around her legs.

'No, I don't. 'S just silly superstition.' Jax crossed his arms. 'Take your hand away.'

'But-' Dit glared.

'Take it away!' He growled, rubbing his eyes.

Slowly, Dit released her pink nose, eyes round with horror.

'Breathe, Dit!' Jax shook her shoulder with a shaky hand.

Taking a gusting breath, she slumped. Her eyelids drooped. 'Oh no.' Shaking, she bent to hold onto her knees. 'Told you...'

The mrug, sensing a game, tried to fly through that gap. It almost knocked her over. She tottered like a doll.

Ky bit his lips, stifling a grin.

'Stupid thing.' Taking her arm, he batted it away.

'Now you've upset it.' Trembling, Dit pointed at its reproachful crimson eyes.

'See! You're fine, Dit.' Jax threw out his arms, staggering.

Ky stared. Jax was always so dignified. He never staggered, or coughed like that.

'I don't think so.' Ky caught his grandmother as she fell. 'Nor are you, Jax.'

His grandfather's eyes were bright red now.

'Oh, Zod's rotting teeth!' Coughing, Jax caught her up, legs buckling. 'Uh-oh.' He danced sideways, tripping on a root. Dit shrieked, knotting her arms round his neck.

'Ha. Enjoy your trip?' Ky caught them before they both fell.

Jax pushed him away, shaking his head.

'We'd better go. I'm sure you can work it out Ky.' With a terse nod, they vanished.

Ky bent over, laughing so hard his ribs hurt.

The mrug settled heavy on his bent back, curious.

Finally, he straightened up. The laughter died.

Now he had to deal with this all on his own.

⋮

High on the hill behind the cabin, turning it all over in his head, he looked down across the broken panorama. Fire scars wriggled black across the shredded, rainbow forests.

Receding floods had left swathes of muddy green. He couldn't see any tmegs.

A ponderous umbo waded through one trail close by, leaving a faint trail of footprints.

The rubble heaps he recycled lay scattered across the plain, skeletal new buildings nearby.

Above, ominous storm clouds clumped in the sky. A warning gust of wind buffeted him, bringing a faint, chemical stink.

Frowning, he looked down, eyes catching on the patterns shifting along the golden pod in his hand.

'Wow.' Mesmerised, he slowly began to feel something there, tickling his consciousness.

Intent, he chased that tickle back to the source. With a spark he connected. A picture formed in his mind.

He jumped up, determined.

'Ky where are you? The squadron has

been summoned.' Fyl's voice made him jump.

What now?

Tugging his ear, he looked for the mrug, called it.

Drifting down, it was still twirling lazy circles. He could see those red eyes watching a flyer busy pecking in a bush.

'Ky?' Fyl sounded anxious.

Chewing his lip, he called it again. The red eyes flicked towards him, then away.

Grinding his teeth, he began to slog through the undergrowth. On his third step, the ground vanished.

He plunged, yelling. Leaves smacked. Twigs scratched. Rocks bruised.

The bushes below caught him. Springing back, they slapped him against a teetering tree. It leaned over with an ominous groan.

Winded, arms tight around a branch, his head swam at the sheer drop beneath his feet. Panting, he waited for his pounding heart to calm. No point calling his dad to get his ear chewed off.

'Ky?' Fyl seemed concerned.

'I'll be there as soon as I can. I have something important to do.' Ky replied, grinding his teeth.

In the haze below, he could see the recent mudslide as a red slash down the hill toward the sliver of river.

The tree leaned further, creaking. His feet swung out into thin air. He scrambled back, hooking them in the branches.

Cold sweat trickled down his neck.

Tempted to peek, the mrug eased into view, grinning above him.

Reaching up both arms he grabbed it, pinging away, the seed-pod driving his destiny.

58

⋮Scream⋮

On a rock-strewn hill at the foot of Panchak the army of healers gathered alongside the Squadron, scanning down the swoop to the plain.

Every eye was focused in the same direction. A grim hush settled.

'The cloud's still growing.' Fyl stated, squinting. His voice bounced off the boulders.

Billowing from the distant canyon, the cloud drifted on the wind, tainting the air, raining pain on the plain in bloody pools.

'Do you really need us, Ty? There are no casualties.' Iyam asked from behind her.

'Not yet. The creatures from the canyon know it's dangerous. Those in its path, don't.' Ty, the chief healer's ragged eyebrows sank over his dark eyes.

'Well, I have to do something.' Iyam stomped off, tugging her braids. 'There's a cave to explore over there.'

'Wait for me.' Eryl joined her.

Fay shuddered, watching the cloud stain spread across the land. It was just like her dream.

Then came the scream.

'Iyam! Eryl!' Fay was the first into the cave, hurtling into the dark.

Without time for her eyes to adjust she ran blind, trying not to think of pombats.

Fumbling too late in her pocket for her blimworm, she tripped.

Her arms flew out. The blimworm slid from her hand.

She fell against a hairy column that smelled of old socks.

Blood turning to ice, she took off like a rocket...

59

⋮Volcano⋮

Sulphur burned his nose, clogged his lungs. Cold stung his battered skin. He perched on a narrow ridge that circled away in both directions behind him. A sea of crumbled rock spread out in every direction.

'This is it.'

Staring down, great, dark swathes snaked away to the moonscape valley. He'd seen pictures of this in a book.

'A volcano. Wow.'

The eerie wail of a lonely eagle rang out. He couldn't spot it. The only other life up here stained the rocks in bright patches of colour.

The mrug wriggled out of his grip, slapping his face.

He stared down at the pod clutched in his hand, waiting for guidance. The music danced light through his head, tingled down his nerves. He was close.

'Ky! Where are you?' Fay's voice hissed in his head.

'It's leading me somewhere. It brought me here.' He transmitted the view, frowning.

His eyes fell on a towering rock stack just above. The pod nudged him toward it. Scrambling up the shifting shale, large lumps rolled and leapt down with every step. He stumbled, slid. Instead of falling from his hand the pod flipped to the back of his hand, as if it were magnetized. The noise was shocking in the silence, rushing away on the breeze.

'I think it's an old volcano.' Looking up, Ky frowned, turning his ankle on a stone. 'Ow!'

'I know the place.' Her voice wheezed in his head. 'I *remember the smell. I'm coming but I may have company.'*

Company?

Behind the stack of rock was a cave. The mrug hovered behind as he staggered inside, into a huge wormhole bored smooth by lava, centuries ago.

As he hobbled down the smooth passage, light filtered through the many holes all around him. Music throbbed from his hand.

'Fay? You inside?' He stopped, resting his feet, sore too where the grit had invaded his sandals.

'Yes. I'm by the waterfall...' Fay sounded breathless. *'I can't see it. Be careful.'*

'Uh? I'm coming...'

He continued down, limping, sucking his furry tongue. The filtered light faded to dimness lit only by the pink bobears on the walls.

Suddenly he could hear a distant, familiar rumble; quickened his pace.

'Where are you?' Fay sounded anxious.

Passing through a wider chamber, he finally burst out into a cavern that soared up into darkness.

'A cavern. Huge. Wow.' Ky stared around.

Hanging high above were uneven stalactites like giant fangs, dripping into puddles on the ground. More fangs rose from the ground to meet them: A dragon's mouth.

Rosy mist hung in the gloom, clinging around the dangling spikes, shadowing the distant edges of the chamber.

The pod sent a delicate chime through his head.

The mrug soared up into the space, excited. There was a crash. He couldn't see what happened. One of the stalactites crashed down close by, exploding into a million pieces.

Ky slapped his hands over his ears. The

gunshot echo throbbed around the cavern as he jumped away from the shower of debris. Agony tore hot through his twisted ankle.

'Ky? Did you do that?' her violin strings whined.

'Stupid mrug.'

That's when he saw it, the print on a patch of dry stone. Long toes, dots at the top, where curved claws just touched. Tmeg!

'Oh no.'

'What?' Did you find it?' Her tone rose higher.

'Hide. Now!'

Guts twisting, Ky turned to run but the music in his head fixed him in place, urging him forward.

Helpless to resist, he stumbled towards the rushing sound, sucking his tongue. Both feet fitted into one toe-joint of the giant footprint.

'Ky? Do you see it?' she screamed.

Grinding his teeth, he limped slowly forward until he could see the waterfall, pouring from the darkness into a midnight pool. Rosy steam tumbled in the humid air.

He stopped, staring down into it, shaking with thirst and terror.

Eel noses stippled the surface for a moment, then sank. His relief was too short. The face of the tmeg solidified beside his reflection, swirling mist. He looked up, gasping, frozen to the spot.

'Ky?' Fay shrieked in his head.

The huge head sank down beside him, snorting dustbin breath. Lit by a thousand bobears, he could see every shimmering scale, every crinkle, spike and claw.

Worst still, he could gaze into those intent, orange eyes and see his snack-size reflection.

'It's here.' He couldn't swallow.

Fay must be able to see it too.

'Yup,' she grated.

His first instinct was to ping. The pod had him in its grasp. He couldn't.

Breathless, he waited for those teeth to

sink into his soft flesh, snap his bones.

Something clacked, above him. It wasn't a tmeg sound. He frowned.

In the pool below, beyond the misty, rippled reflection of the tmeg, he made out pinpricks of light and behind, the stabwebber crouching on the ceiling.

His stomach clenched. He felt sick.

'Oh no.' He closed his eyes, drowning in the scent of rotting meat and old socks. Thundering water filled his ears.

'Ping!' Fay screamed, piercing his brain.

'You know I can't.' He shook his head, tugging his ear, tasting ashes.

60

┇Fang┇

Looking up, Fay's view beyond the cascade was obscured by tmeg scales.

'Ky?' Breath fluttering, she backed further into the darkness.

Too far.

The ground vanished beneath her feet. She plunged, gasping into thin air.

'Aah!' It felt like being swallowed. Her blue fingernails shredded as she scrabbled for a grip on the rocky throat.

'Fay?' Ky's voice filled her head.

She slid, scraping her shoulders and head. Bumping down over ridges and lumps, a sense of space burst around her.

A watery gurgle filled the air. She fell into soft surprise, panting.

'You alright?' His voice was a comfort in the pitch dark.

Jutting her chin, she mustn't think about pombats.

'Think so. Just fell down a hole. Landed in something soft.' Grimacing, she rubbed the grains between her fingers, unable to resist sniffing. *'Mouldy sand, I think.'*

'Sounds like you're safer there. It's a stand-off up here.' He sounded grim.

'Ha. Can't see a way back anyway.' She reached for a handful of dark, swinging her hand around.

'Call your mrug. They see well in the dark. I'll find you when it's over. Gotta go.' He cut off.

Clenching her grubby fists, Fay summoned her mrug, seeking out any other life nearby.

There was nothing more than the beasts above.

Shuffling she groped about, waiting for the mrug. Maybe it couldn't find her. Perhaps it didn't want to...

Finally, something dropped over her head. A mrug hug! They shared a moment of joy, until she needed to breathe.

She connected fully as she peeled it away. Sending it up, the cavern grew before her as it drifted away, clear as daylight. The roof soared away into the gloom, the point of the odd stalactite bright as the tip of a fang.

Pombats would roost up there.

Gulping, she turned back, found the shaft she'd fallen down and began to climb.

Finally, she popped out behind the waterfall, in time to see the cornered stabwebber poised to attack. It was gibbering like a monkey in a cloud of tiny lights.

Strange, unfamiliar power swirled in the air, electric.

Her curious mrug drifted towards it. She called it back.

All three stabbers lanced down toward Ky, standing defenceless by the pool.

'Ky!' Her scream fled into the dark. Her pearly nails flashed as her hand covered her mouth.

She couldn't watch.

61

⫶Claws⫶

One stabber sparked off the rock between Ky and the tmeg. Fay's shriek rang off the walls. He jumped, feeling the rush of air past his cheek as another stab just missed.

The tmeg rumbled, rattling its wings.

'Dad! Help!' Ky leapt away, teeth gritting against the pain in his ankle.

Roaring, the tmeg reared up on its hind legs, slashing at furry legs and pincers. The stabwebber's tiny lights turned angry red, jiggling.

One giant, sweeping claw almost robbed him of his leg as the beast fought to grab the webber.

Hopping away, Ky covered his ears as the tmeg's grumble rolled over him, warring with vibration from the webber.

He slid under cover of a jagged rock.

Bellowing, the tmeg yanked at claws and furry legs. Stabbers darted around it. The stabwebber rattled, claws thrashing, falling to the ground. A gust of vinegar and old socks blasted up, coating his tongue.

For a moment, Ky caught a close-up view of one of its fly eyes. Too close. The vibrations hurt his ears.

Then, wounded, it was dragging itself away.

The stabwebber's gibber and hiss was lost against the screech of the angry tmeg echoing around the cavern.

Ky scuttled behind a boulder, holding his

breath. Ears covered tight, he rolled into a ball.

'Dad! Help!' he sent again, rocking, hopeless.

Minutes passed, like years. The stabwebber retreated back to the roof.

The tmeg bellowed, tormented by the vibrations in its ears.

A webber claw, ripped from its limb, bounced over Ky's head. A mangled stabber landed right in front of him, still twitching. He stared at it, chilled.

'Dad, where are you?' Ky tried again, shaking. There was still no reply.

'You're never there!' he yelled, curling his fingers into fists. As ever, he was on his own.

He pulled out his phone, face burning. The din was so loud its sounds would have no impact. He could record it, though. Tapping it on, he shoved it away again.

'Fay where are you?'

'Hiding, like you.' she quailed. *'I think it heard me. Maybe it's a Listener.'*

B. Random

Ky tugged his ear, hard. Soon, the tmeg would win, Listener or not. The shivering stabwebber was just defending itself. Fay and he would be lunch for the victor.

Leaping to swipe at the webber limping away on the roof, the tmeg crashed to the ground by his refuge. Flailing and screaming its claws scoured rock just above his head. It yanked a stabber out of its eye, rocking on its feet.

Shaking its fur with a deep rustling sound, the stabwebber lowered itself on a thick strand of web. Tiny red lights danced around it. Keening, dodging the roaring, swiping tmeg, it swung towards a hole half way up the cavern wall.

Rustling, it gathered its broken legs and leapt for safety. Catching the lip of the hole with its good legs, it dragged the rest in behind it, leaving dark smears on the rock. The lights vanished with it. The sizzling rush of sparking power faded from the cavern.

Fay's mrug drifted after it. His followed,

408

its old scars shining in the gloom. Hovering at a safe distance from the hole, his sent a flyer's eye view of the stabwebber he could do without, all bristles and legs.

Sudden silence slammed down. He shook his head, sure he'd gone deaf. It was over. His phone bleeped, battery flat. That would be the recording of a lifetime. He smiled.

The pod chimed again through his mind.

Dizzy from lack of air, he peeked out. There was no sign of the stabwebber. The battered tmeg lay dog-like, soaking up the puddles. Both eyes were half closed, one trickling a dark trail of blood or poison. A punctured wing hung askew from its back.

The mrug draped over its forehead. Maybe it understood, but he didn't.

'Ky? You alright?'

'So far. The tmeg's right beside me. Did you see where the stabwebber went?'

Slowly, he climbed back to his throbbing feet.

'No. I had my eyes closed. It's injured.'

Shuddering, he sidled a step away, then another. The tmeg didn't move, ragged breathing blasting through his hair.

'The tmeg's hurt bad too.' Fay sent.

'Poisoned, I expect. It took a stabber in the eye.'

Ky, the pod's chiming insistent now, crept on. Finally, he scuttled around the edge of the pool.

With a dubious glance back, unable to swallow, he clambered behind the waterfall.

Fay was suddenly in front of him.

'There you are!' A hug seemed a really good idea.

'Was that the same stabwebber?' Ky let go, feeling his ears burn.

'Think so.' She nodded, twisting her lips.

'Is it dead?'

Fay's eyes took on a far-away look.

'No. Hurt. Licking its wounds. Poor thing.' She gazed up at the hole. 'I should heal it.'

'Are you nuts!?' Ky held up the pod. 'The music's ringing loud in my head here. This must be the place.'

'Well, you deal with that. I need to go heal the tmeg. It's failing.' Fay strode away, rubbing her shoulder.

'Be careful!' Ky yelled at her retreating back. It might be hurt, but it could still be hungry. 'Fay. Wait.'

He tried to set down the pod, failed. Fay trotted away. His feet wouldn't follow. Frowning, he stared at it, scratching his head. The music faded as he turned to watch.

Fay was crouched beside the tmeg. She looked so tiny, the size of one long nostril. That weird straight hair tailed across the floor. Head bowed, her hands were working their magic. The tmeg didn't twitch.

Chewing his lip, he stepped further into the gloom. The chiming changed to a merry tinkling.

Slowly, the pod began to crack open, revealing four shining, silver seeds inside.

His mrug sailed past, drifting after Fay into the cavern. He watched her with one eye through their link.

One at a time, he set the seeds in damp crevices either side of the falls. Their high, eager tinkling rang through his head.

Finally the pod was empty.

'Is that what you wanted?' Ky scratched his head, holding up his sore foot.

'Ky! Come help me.' Her calm voice was back to normal. He smiled. The seeds' happy music was infectious.

'I'm coming.' He gazed at the seed pod.

The patterns swirled red. With a sound like a peal of bells, the whole pod withered black, turning to dust in his fingers.

Flapping off the dust as he left, Ky looked down to see the trumpet shape of the flower etched into the palm of his hand. He rubbed it, but it was set there, like a scar. Ky scowled. It wasn't the sort of tattoo he'd have chosen.

Back in the cavern, the tmeg snores rang off the walls.

Fay, eyes closed, had her hands on its huge head.

'What can I do?' He limped forward.

Silent, she grabbed one of his hands, setting it on hers. Ky did the same with the other, marked hand, setting it over hers on the broken scales.

The tmeg's breath stank, gushing around them. Sharing their link, Ky felt the poison coursing through the veins, pouring from its wounds.

Dropping to his knees, he felt muscle and sinew mend, the eye sealing back into its socket. Looking down he spotted one of the webber's spines lodged between its teeth. Cautious, he kicked it out.

Leaning against the heaving ribs, as he felt their power wane, he helped knit the wings back together.

'That's it,' whispered Fay after an eternity, rocking back on her heels, glancing back at the hole. 'We can leave him to sleep it off now. Nothing left in the tank to heal the webber anyway. Besides, it's gone.'

'I'm starving! And so thirsty!' His legs

wobbled as he stood.

'We need to wash off any poison.' Fay stumbled toward the pool.

Far from the tmeg, relief made him sag at the edge of the fall.

'Don't-' Ky leant forward, swinging an arm.

'There's no sign of the eels.' Fay leaned down, washing, then flapping her hands.

After a dubious moment, he snatched water with both hands, drinking until the shaking stopped. She did the same.

The mrug joined him at the edge, drinking too. Ky watched its eyes bulge as it swallowed.

Fay's mrug plunged fearless into the pool.

'I'm still hungry.' His stomach growled in time with hers. Fay giggled.

'Me too. Now you know why there's healers' bread. But we have to go back.' She shook her head.

'Go back where?'

'The cliff. If that cloud rains over this mountain, those seeds will be in real danger so close to the waterfall. You will too, if the Listeners decide to blame you.'

'Oh no! Let's go.' Ky grabbed her hand. They vanished.

Unseen, behind them in the cavern, the yawning tmeg vanished too.

62

⋮Splats⋮

Fay's healers were gone from the cliff. Instead, the cloud hovered directly above their rocky bluff.

Something thumped behind them as voices screamed a warning.

'Ping!' yelled Fay.

Ky grabbed her hand. They bounced again. Not far enough.

They were in the bottom of the valley,

sinking.

The healed tmeg plopped in beside them, groaning. Flying splats smacked both of them in the face.

'Urgh!' Ky spat, scraping it out of his eyes. 'What is this stuff? It reeks.'

'Jellysand. Ew.' Fay scraped olive goop from her hair, smearing it down her nose. 'Help!' she yelled, sinking.

The more she thrashed, the more she sank. It was past her knees already.

'Like quicksand but slower, I hope?' Ky frowned.

'Doesn't feel slow.' Fay waved her arms for balance, panting. 'Feels much too quick to me.'

The tmeg stretched out as long as its body would go. It watched them from its good eye, the other still visibly mending.

'Keep still,' urged Ky, watching the tmeg. A bead of sweat slid down his face.

Fay looked up, gulping.

'Oh no. We're still under the cloud.' She

struggled, sinking further. Two flakes had been sore enough. She didn't want to burn again.

'Stop wiggling. We need a plank or a rope. I saw this in a movie once.' Ky was still staring at the tmeg.

'And these are likely to be laying around in a desert?' scoffed Fay. 'Just ping.'

She struggled to wind up her power. She could feel his sparking feeble static around hers.

'Ready?'

'Go.' Ky nodded. They let it blast. Nothing happened.

'Again.' Fay clamped her jaw, winding it up.

Nothing.

The crowd on the hill yelled encouragement.

'Must be something to do with the quicksand.' Ky muttered.

'Nope. I said there was nothing left in the tank. Looks like we pinged the tmeg. It's definitely all gone.' Fay groaned, sinking to her waist. Her teeth were beginning to chatter now, despite the feeble sun.

'We pinged the tmeg? I don't believe this. First the webber and now the tmeg. What's going on?' wailed Ky.

Fay eyed the huge creature stretched out nearby. Eyes fixed upon them, its hunger rolled over her.

'If we get out, the tmeg will eat us,' she muttered.

'Great. I don't see our friends rushing to our aid, either.' Ky grumbled, glancing up the hill.

'Fyl can you help? We pinged the tmeg. Power's gone.' Fay sent, fighting to raise her knees.

'We'll try the mrugs.'

'They're bringing the squadron!' She waved as the mrugs lifted from the hill. 'Look!'

The squadron sailed overhead, diamond shadows drifting across the plain.

419

Ky's mrug zoomed down, hovering above. He reached up to grab the tendrils. The mrug tugged him up.

Fyl reached down to her, yanking her up by the hand, her mrug bobbing above. She moved up maybe the width of her hand. The sticky, khaki muck clung to her feet.

'Try again!' yelled Fyl, circling overhead.

Glancing around, she saw Ky lifting and sliding, pulled by his mrug. Jutting her chin she glared at hers, too small to be of any use. With an offended sniff, it floated away.

Fyl reached down again, grabbing her tunic, heaving. Tytus joined him.

'Pull your kneeth up!' Tytus yelled as his mrug sank beneath him. Fyl too, took the strain, muscles bulging in his arms. The mrugs were almost flat to the surface now.

Suddenly, her feet slipped free. She found herself sliding out, head down, one arm flapping.

From the corner of her eye she saw Ky sliding too.

'Wait! Stop!' he yelled, suddenly bumping against a wall of green scales. Releasing his grip on the mrug, he landed on a giant, clawed foot.

Jaw dropping as she slid, Fay watched him slowly raise his head to gaze into that huge orange eye. Fabric ripped, she dropped.

'Ah! Run Ky!' she cried, taking a mouthful of goo.

Blinking, confused, he looked at her.

'No more,' he muttered, standing on the scaly foot.

'Urgh!' Spitting sand, rolling onto solid ground, she sat up to look. 'No Ky! It's hungrier than us,' she squawked as he clambered up towards the tmeg's shoulder.

'I know what I'm doing, Fay.' Ky climbed higher. *'Hey, look after my phone, will you?'* He tossed it toward her. She caught it.

'Oh no,' Fyl gasped, above her. With a flick of his hand he called the squadron together, snatching her up.

Dropping her with the healers, they flew

cautious circles above.

'Iyam, Eryl! I was so worried!' They helped Fay to her feet, brushing at her clothes.

'There's a farm down there!' someone barked, shielding their eyes. 'Look!'

All eyes but Fay's, swivelled to the path of the growing cloud. The nearest field turned as maroon as dried blood in its shadow.

Fay glanced at the dark rain slicing the sky, sucking her teeth. Her hands flew up to her cheeks. 'Luna's prediction. It's happening, all of it.'

The squadron zoomed away. Winking, Fay's mrug went with them.

Pausing for breath at the top of a scaly leg, Ky shaded his eyes to watch the team. He climbed slowly higher, over the base of the wing.

Fay stared, tasting ash. The tmeg hadn't moved, still stretched out flat, eyes drifting closed.

She slid her hands over her mouth. Soon he would be close enough for an easy snap of those teeth. Another wave of its seething hunger washed over her.

'Ky, you can't!' she wailed, through her fingers. There was nothing the squadron would be able to do.

'Ky, don't! Please.' Hopeless, she closed her eyes, trying to swallow. Life stretched away, eternally grey without her best friend.

She opened them again at the sound of the tmeg moving. It rose to its feet, creaking scales, shuffling healed wings. Everyone stepped back. Fingers blocking her view, she almost missed Ky, clambering towards its neck.

'No choice, Fay,' he sent, grabbing for hand-holds.

Fay couldn't swallow. Her heartbeat crashed on her ribs. He was going to vanish into that huge, hungry mouth any second, for sure.

She jumped as the tmeg tipped its head up. Clarion sound spiralled away into the air...

63

⫶Charge⫶

All Ky could hear was his insane heart, thumping loud in his ears. Breath wheezed through his dry throat. His eyes hurt from the pictures blinking into his head, urging him up.

He felt its immense mind absorb his view of the crisis; so many silver flakes swishing away past planets spinning through space.

Understanding settled, solidifying between them.

Reeling, Ky clamped pale lips.

'Ah!' His flimsy sandals slid on the glossy scales, stabbing daggers through his ankle. Leg swinging, puffing, he clung on. 'Don't look down. Don't look down.'

Wedging his tortured fingers under another gold-edged scale, he hoisted himself up. In the shadow of the row of spikes at the top, he gritted his teeth.

Huffing, he reached up again, digging in his toes.

Tipping its giant head back, the tmeg bellowed. Ears ringing, swinging out, he grabbed higher, heaving himself up.

The delicate wing felt warm, soft under his fingers, sparkling in the sun. Long spars between sections, flexed their whippy points, almost ripping off his arm.

He froze as the wing twitched. Had it changed its mind? Had he hurt it?

The tmeg turned its giant head to look back at him. Its fangs almost grazed his face, foul breath making his stomach heave.

425

Gulping, his eyes locked on one giant orange orb. The tmeg's vast consciousness yawned, big as a galaxy, inside his head.

'It knows,' Ky sent, teeth rattling as their minds merged.

Pictures thundered through his brain like a movie run at a million miles per hour. Reality fled, squeezed out, shrieking. It was like being run over by a bus. He dare not let go to hold his exploding head.

'Wow,' he muttered, dizzy.

The tmeg lurched to its feet. Gasping, digging in as it rocked, he grabbed its neck, tucking each hand under an up-curving scale at the crest. Hooking a leg around the bottom of a spike he settled to the hard, rough circle of bumps at its base, grimacing.

The tmeg turned, its lashing tail shredding bushes. Crouching, it leapt into the air, spreading out its freshly-healed wings to glide.

Unprepared, still entranced, Ky gasped in the whoosh of air. Flailing, eyes popping, he

426

clung on.

His fingers slipped. One leg flew out. Every sinew strained as he dragged himself back into position. Gasping, he tucked his knees in, curled his fingers back under scales.

The vastness of the tmeg's mind still held him, plotting. Straining for a thought of his own, he fought to focus, awash in dark, flashing space.

Wind blasted through his lips, inflating his cheeks. Yanking at the roots, hair flew, lashed. His eyelids flapped, stinging. His bottom on the bumps was beginning to burn.

Once aloft, the tmeg circled the jellysand patch, huffing. Ky's lips returned to his teeth.

He snatched his mind from the tmeg's. Turning his head, he looked down.

His faithful mrug was right behind, following. He grinned.

'No! Go back to Fay!' He sent, catching the defiant gleam in its eyes. *'They need you for the squadron. Go to them.'*

Its scarlet eyes stared into his. Then it flipped up a wing, turning away, squirting poo in a silent comment. Ky sighed his relief.

Fay was down there, watching, one hand on her head, mouth a black hole. He didn't dare wave.

One swamping second of connection had been enough to see its true nature. In that moment, as he settled on its neck, he'd shared the wisdom of ages and the danger of the growing cloud.

The tmeg understood, but seemed only able to communicate in these deep, searing flashes. Maybe it was a Listener.

Ky jumped as the tmeg bellowed.

Looking up, he saw armies flying in from every direction. More tmegs emerged from the forests, the mountains, the hazy distance. Thousands of them.

His stomach did a flip.

Hanging on, feet scrabbling, he watched the first tmeg land below, scattering the squadron. It began clawing at the jellysand, scooping it into its mouth.

Other tmegs came to join it, feasting in the bog.

Now he couldn't see the ground. Green scales of every tone, tall spikes and flapping gold or copper wings had taken over.

Soon there was a miles-wide funnel of flying tmegs soaring around them, reaching high into the sky.

He kicked his legs to urge the tmeg forward. Nothing changed. He tried to make that connection again, but that didn't work either. They kept circling.

Finally, once there was room on the ground, his tmeg landed to take its fill too. He swung on the spike as they landed, nearly spilling off.

Now he was surrounded.

Muscles bunching under green scales, flashing wings and fangs blurred all around him. He gagged at the stench.

Necks dipped and bulged beside him. His heart was drumming on his ribs. He felt like a flea on a dog.

Suddenly, neighbouring tmegs leaned over him. Before he could duck, they vomited the chewed jellysand all over him. It stank even worse.

'Ugh!' He shuddered as the cold soaked through his tunic. 'Why would you do that? Why?'

He flailed his arms, before they could dump it over him again.

They were re-filling, jumping away into the sky.

Catching laughter on the wind, Ky felt his ears burn.

He scraped his eyes clear as gobs of tmeg sick dripped off his head. Squinting, he couldn't make out Fay in the crowd.

He gave the tmeg a grumpy kick. It gathered itself to leap.

'Wahoo!' This time, Ky was more prepared for the effects of take-off. 'Let's do this!'

Then he was shooting toward the boiling cloud like a missile.

Smarting eyes caught a glimpse of the squadron, rushing off.

Heat seared his cheeks, his chest. His dangling, clogged fringe made a shield. Filthy fingers, gripping tight, hurt as he yelled.

'Charge!'

Suddenly, a current flowed between them. His every thought was shared and valued. He knew every instinct, every movement before the tmeg made it, swirling in the drilling darkness of connection.

They were as one, as the tmeg flapped toward the cloud. The rhythm beat through his veins. There was no fear, no doubt.

It trumpeted a battle cry, lunging forward with a powerful surge.

Ky roared along with it, gripping tight with knees and fingers.

Bellowing, the tmeg army followed, swooping and diving after them.

Ky ducked his head as they plunged into the bitter fog. Every breath choked.

The tmeg seemed to swell beneath him,

431

contracting as it belched purple fire.

Heat billowed over him, searing his chest where the jellysand had missed. He hunched closer to the spike.

The cloud turned to tatters, shredding before his wondering eyes.

Wings beat around him, thumping the air.

He felt the ribs beneath his heels spread, then pull in. Again, purple flame jetted from between those fangs.

A clawed foot whistled over his head.

A dreadful, acrid stench, worse than the jellysand or the cloud, engulfed him.

Looking back, the tmeg behind took clods of brown in the face. Poo too? Oh no.

Lips clamped, Ky's head whipped round. The tmeg to his right blew fire. Sure enough, there it came, shooting past.

'Yuk.' He ducked deeper behind the spike, scanning ahead for the next volley as they swooped higher.

Blasts of magenta swirled the cloud from lace to vanishing haze. Foul clods and sprays whizzed like missiles around him.

Squinting against the wind, he saw patches of clear sky emerge. The cloud was fizzling away. In clean patches, he huffed a breath.

He glanced down, past scaled, sinuous bodies and flapping wings. His tmeg jinked. The sliver of river he glimpsed, winding through the rainbow forest tilted, made his head spin.

He looked up instead, took a splat in the eye.

Tmegs blurred around him, diving and twisting, fast as fish.

He closed that eye, clamped his mouth. Squinting, he curled filthy fingers tight.

Blasting their magical fire, swinging long necks, they'd burn him any second too.

His mount dived and twisted like some out-of-control fairground ride. Sharing the tmeg's mind, all he could think of was clearing that cloud.

Ky clung on, spine screaming, legs

cramping, waiting for his next breath.

Tmeg-wing shadows flashed around him. One spun the air, brushing his cheek. He ducked.

Peering down again as the hazy, rainbow forest swung far below, he shut his eyes.

He'd yearned to fly all his life. He tried a whoop, failed. This was nothing like riding the mrug.

If he slid off now, the tmeg wouldn't even notice.

64

⋮Hero⋮

Up on the hill, Fay clapped her hand over her lips, watching Ky swoop away on his tmeg. None of the Legends she'd ever heard, told of a boy who rode a tmeg. Ky was re-writing history, whether he lived or died. She blinked away the sting of tears as the tmeg army vanished into those poisonous billows above.

'The cloud's moving again, fast in this

wind and look it's still growing.' Fyl pointed, frowning at the towering cloud, now shadowing the farm on the horizon.

Her mrug circled, winking, then zipped away.

Fay stared at the smoking stones and bones that were all that remained of a closer farmstead the cloud passed earlier. The stench drifted on the fickle wind.

This poisoned rain would seep through the ground, even into the caves.

Through her mrug's keen eyes, she saw there were people outside a distant farm, looking up. They began to run.

Through the mrug, Fay's special sense extended out to them.

'It's Myn's family!' She slapped her hands to her head. 'The cloud's raining on their front yard.'

'Let's fly.' Fyl leapt onto his mrug. 'That cloud's too unpredictable. Pinging could put us all in danger.'

Mounting up, the squadron shot away.

Fay's gaze returned to the farm. Her mrug was above it now, its special eyes giving her a clear view.

Out of the blue, behind the family came a whirlwind. Fry, in its pyjamas leapt on the larger figure's head. Fighting to get it off, they staggered forward into the rain, the others screaming behind. Chilling, the shrieks carried up the valley.

In the breathless silence, Fay couldn't rip her eyes away.

Fry clung on, spread like a coat over head and shoulders as they ran.

'I don't believe it. Fry's trying to protect them,' she croaked, digging blue nails in her palms.

'Fry? The mad kittle?' someone snorted.

'What's it wearing?' Uneasy titters trickled out.

'Sacrificing itself?' came a whisper.

'Like a gaut?' A derisive honk pierced the hush.

'Exactly like a gaut.' Fay smiled,

437

remembering the cape they'd used to make the pyjamas.

The squadron had scooped up the figure at the far edge of the cloud now.

Fry was prancing back for the next, repeating its mission. On the second run, its pale pyjamas were looking pink.

When Fry finally returned to leap on screaming Myn, the frills were beginning to smoke.

Now the crowd on the hill began hooting; hollering encouragement.

Wailing, Myn ran, tripping and stumbling. Deep in the cloud, bonnet bobbing, Fry clung on.

By the time they reached the squadron, Fry's pyjamas were beginning to shred. Slices flapped down as he bounced.

Grabbing him, Myn climbed aboard Byran's mrug. The kittle shrieked, thrashing as they floated back to the hill. Myn clung on tight.

Her pale little mrug flew right alongside

all the way back. Fay smothered a smug grin.

'It's hurt.' She rushed over to Byran's landing mrug.

'Please help it Fay. It saved us.' Myn's eyes were full of tears as she handed the kittle over.

Fay peeled away the smoking pyjamas. Fry quivered, drooling.

'Come on team, we have some healing to do,' she said, rubbing her hands.

None of them took time to marvel as the sky turned bright with the tmegs' purple flames.

65

⁝Luck⁝

Circling, the giant tmeg roared its satisfaction. Around them spun a whirlwind of wings.

Shuddering, Ky clung to the spike, shaking with strain.

His face, arms and legs were numb. He couldn't wait to be rid of the thundering pain of their connection.

The tmeg army began to disperse,

trumpeting into the distance. Gold and copper flashed in the waning sunlight.

It was a scene of fantasy beyond his imaginings, like the terrifying beauty of the purple fire that had saved them.

With the tmeg's final belch, the final wisp of cloud melted into the wind. Turning its long head, the tmeg winked at him, glancing down.

Ky stared down at the lake below. It had to be the same tmeg that chased him all that time ago. It knew.

Staring into that huge, burning eye, a million images streaming through his brain, he chased one idea down, nodding. A swim would remove his stinking, itching crust.

One huge wing snapped up like a sail. Sliding, Ky had to hang on tight as it zoomed down toward the water.

Straining, he glanced round, spotting his faithful mrug cruising towards him. No friendly corner would tip up to stop him sliding on this ride. He gazed at the mrug, feeling his bottom burn, yearning for that soft, warm platform to ride.

With a snort, perhaps of outrage if it was reading his mind, the tmeg shook him off like a flea.

'Aah!' His exhausted arms gave out. Yelping he fell, flapping, tumbling.

A burst of sound filled his ears. It sounded suspiciously like laughter as the tmeg shot away.

The hollow log from his nightmares was still rocking in the shallows. With typical bad luck, Ky crash-landed right there.

He bounced, limp, into the water. The world turned off.

⋮

His eyelid drifted slowly up. Fay's was the first face he saw. Her healing hands still glowed hot on his chest.

'Welcome back.' She rocked onto her heels, removing that welcome warmth.

'What-?' He croaked, rubbing his sore

throat, his clogged eye.

'Your mrug saved the day. Scooped you out the lake, brought you to me.' Fay smiled, glancing up as the diamond shadow fell over him.

Struggling to sit up in the grass, the mrug dropped over his head in a hug. Ky stroked it grinning, feeling that special bond between them grow.

'I'd always prefer to ride you,' he whispered, peeling its heavy bulk away after a squeeze. It floated up to hover just above him, broadcasting joy.

'I owe you Fay. Can't believe I'm still alive.' Wincing, Ky rubbed his stomach through the charred remains of his tunic. He peered around the friends staring down at him. 'The flames were all round me.'

'That makes two of us.' Fay shivered, 'I keep blocking out the image of your tiny figure perched on that spike at the front of the charge.'

'Ha. It wasn't comfortable.' Ky was

suddenly aware that his behind no longer throbbed. He smiled at her.

'C'mon let's fuel up.' She held out a hand, pulling him up, swinging back her long hair.

Central Eating was full, everyone celebrating their eventful day.

With full shells, Fay and Ky settled at the end of a rough bench under the shelter. He sat down gently, smiling at her when there was no discomfort. The mrug hovered close by.

A powerful barbeque scent from the griddles hung in the cooling air. His mouth watered.

'You're insane. No way I'd climb on a tmeg's back. Too close to the teeth.' Tem shuddered, waving his crust.

'We'd just healed it. It was starving hungry. I was sure it would snap him up.' Fay shivered, picking at her stew with those weird blue nails.

'No choice.' Ky shrugged, scooping a hasty mouthful from his shell. 'I have to admit to a wobble though, as the last patches dissolved, when I could suddenly see how far I could fall.'

'You could have run away.' Zay, Dav's friend, piped up.

'I just did what had to be done,' Ky mumbled, shaking his soggy head. 'Running away doesn't solve anything.'

A crowd had collected around him, standing, perched on tables or sitting by his feet, dunking or chewing.

'Why wasn't your back burnt?' Dav asked, nibbling cubes.

'The tmegs sicked up jellysand all over him,' replied Fyl, slapping him on the back.

'Better wash your hand now, Fyl,' Fay urged, grinning. 'That cloud was poison too.'

'Ugh.' Holding out his hand, Fyl hurried off to the waterfall.

'Worse than that. They poop as they blow fire.' A shower of blackened globs burst from Ky's wet hair as he shook his head.

'Ewww!' The children hooted and giggled.

445

'Great job, Ky. Jellysand must have more special properties than we realised.' Voyn nodded, approaching with Fay's Ma. 'I will be looking into that. It was helpful that the tmegs filled the source crack with it when they'd finished. Looks like they'd burnt the jellysand to a sort of black cement.'

Voyn settled close by to eat, handing his partner her bowl.

'They did? I didn't see.' Chewing, Ky scratched his head, grimacing at his grimy wet fingers. 'Even after a dip in the lake, I still need a bath.' Holding out his sticky digits, he stopped talking to fill up on food again with his cleaner hand.

'What's that?' Dav pointed at his grimy hand. The flower on his palm glowed, livid.

'It's my new tattoo. Like it?' Ky grimaced.

'Not very heroic, is it?' Dav considered, head tilted over.

'Sloppy.' Zay shook his head. 'Hey, it's the same as Fay's clip.'

'So it is. But you really don't smell like a

flower even after a dip.' Fay wrinkled her nose, smiling. Ky glared at her.

A familiar shape pranced towards her.

'Fry!' The kittle bounced into her arms.

'Fry you behave,' Myn yelled, chasing behind. 'Oh, it's you, Fay. Pananas. Fry is so special isn't it?' Myn beamed.

'Every creature is special. At least it kept its tufts of new fur.' Fay nodded, stroking under Fry's downy ear. Its back legs twitched with pleasure.

Ky stared at Fay. His whole story was there, pinned to her tunic. She knew, all along, as usual.

'Fry's hungry, like me.' Waving at her calling parents, Myn headed off toward the food queue, passing Fyl on the way.

'How long will it be before she realises she left Fry behind?' Fay grinned. Fry sneezed.

The squadron sat ranged around them, like family.

'Who'd have thought Fry would turn out

to be a hero?' Fay spoke loud, winking at Ky.

Hands reached in all around her to pet the kittle. There was a chorus of cooing. Fry's happy tongue licked and slobbered.

Ky smiled, intent on filling his mouth.

'Suddenly I'm starving.' Eyes flicking from the kittle to the friends all around her, Fay finally began to scoop up food with hungry fingers.

Smiling, Ky watched the blue tint fade from her fingernails, her hair springing up into wild curls. 'Wow.'

Frowning, she scratched her head, pulling a curl around to stare. Holding out her hands, she turned her fingers to the light.

'Guess I'm back to normal.' She met his eyes, sharing a smile. 'Oh, here's your phone.'

A shadow cut off the dying sun.

Looking up, Ky met Dad's eyes, squaring his shoulders.

Fay's wary eyes flicked from one to the other. Beside Balzar, Voyn was joined by Iago and Gwyn. A crowd of other Elders stood by their table, back-lit green by some of the Ancients.

Ky nodded at his dad, chewing deliberately but suddenly not tasting. He should have found time to speak to him.

'None of us true Mraxi could have done what you did, because of the effect of the plant. Evidently, you were destined to be here.' Iago grinned. 'I hear Zod has marked you.'

Ky frowned, confused, then held up his tender palm.

'No-one has ridden a tmeg before either.' Put in Voyn, smiling as he chewed.

Grimacing, Ky glimpsed his mrug snatching a flyer from the air behind him, the faithful shadow of Fay's right beside it.

'Wasn't exactly comfortable.' He shifted his behind on the bench.

'Bravery rarely is.' Grandad Jax smiled at him from the back. Beside him, Gwyn nodded, smiling.

'So, the tmegs, the eels won't bother me

again?' Ky gulped his last mouthful.

'You completed the task.' Iago assured him, winking at Fay. 'They will revert to listening as before.'

'Maybe I can sleep again, then.' He sighed. 'But I can't take all the credit. It was Fay who saw that the seeds were ready to grow. If we hadn't realised that...'

'Fay's part will be recognised, don't concern yourself.' Voyn nodded, patting Fay's bows. 'The stress has receded, I see. Good.'

'Cool.' Nodding, Ky took another mouthful, staring at his silent father.

'I knew you could do it, Fay. This is just the beginning for you.' Voyn puffed out his chest, rubbing her shoulder.

Ky could hear her grinding her teeth. The word 'beginning' had an ominous ring to it.

'Wonderful! The Chime will flourish, and the cloud threat is gone, thanks to you.' Iago bobbed a little bow to each of them.

'Where did the cloud come from?' Ky asked, eyeing Fay's jutting chin.

'Since the change in our orbit, the planet's crust plates are moving more which is why we are having these earthquakes. One such quake during an eclipse, drained the Sour Sea. The chemicals mixing with the lava beneath created the gas cloud,' Boyng explained from beside Jax.

'Healers needed. Urgent. Injured giant stabwebber.' The call clanged through everyone's head.

'Ours?' He smiled at Fay.

'Has to be.' She leapt to her feet, eager to escape. He could feel the sizzle of her power winding up.

'Fay, I owe you.' He reached out. *'Careful.'*

Grinning she touched his hand with cold fingertips. She waved as she vanished.

Ky met his dad's sharp stare.

'It caused a lot of damage. We need to restore life to great swathes of land. We're working on it already.' Iago rubbed his hands together.

'Great.' Ky nodded, only listening with half

an ear, his eyes fixed on his father.

'We won't forget Ky. Mrax is in your debt.' Bowing, the Elders began to vanish.

Soon everyone was blurring from sight.

'Well, we need to patrol once more, just to make sure everything is back to normal.' Fyl stood away from the table, looking awkward. The other boys joined him, eyes flicking between them.

'I'll catch up with you.' Ky turned, reaching up to touch the mrug.

Arms folded, Balzar stared fiercely at him until they'd all gone.

'I can't excuse what you did.' Balzar bit out, scowling.

'I should have-.' Pale, Ky rose to his feet, jutting his chin.

'But I do understand now I've seen your mother.' Balzar's face broke into a wry smile. 'She needs me a lot more than the Ancients do. I see that now. I won't leave her here again, you have my word.'

'Good.' Ky gulped. 'Stick to it.'

'Proud of you, son.' Dad hugged him, hard.

A little glow replaced the chunk of ice inside him as he pulled away.

'So where's Mum?' He sniped.

'I left her on Earth, for now. She has a few issues to resolve.' Balzar scratched his guilty forehead, looking away.

Those issues could take a while to fix. Nightmares about the stabwebber on Earth still haunted him too. He knew just how his dad felt.

'Probably best.' Ky nodded. 'I need to go...'

Balzar stood back, bowing his head. 'Fancy going fishing Ky?' He shrugged in the silence. 'It won't be like Earth fishing but I've a lot of catching up to do.'

'Absolutely.' Ky's heart flipped.

Their eyes met. They shared a smile.

His mrug drifted lazy circles beside him. Grasping its tendrils, he swung onto its scarred back. Swooping up into the sky, he scanned for movement between the trees.

'Wahoo!' he cried, settling into the comfort of their bond as they soared. 'This is proper flying! See you in the morning, Dad, after squadron.'

That grin was never going to leave his face.

THE END

About the Author

B. Random lives with family and fish near the coast. She loves reading, travel, sunshine, wildlife and live music.

Her passion for sci-fi and fantasy developed as a teenager. Membership of the local writer's society has led to and a warm, supportive circle of lasting friendships. Her inspirations come from wild country and the sea.

The appeal of living in another world, escaping from the mundane, endures. Her ability to create worlds full of surprises is a gift. To build interesting characters, she combines observation and empathy so they take on their own personalities. Her creatures are flights of pure imagination. As a writer, her final reward is to introduce readers to that brand new world and show them its magic.

If you have enjoyed this book, please share a good review.

To sign up for the newsletter and find out when new books are coming out, please visit the website at www.b-random.space. There will be more, soon.

B. Random